6/09

D0114614

HELEN
GARNER

The
Spare
Room

ANANSI

First published in 2008 by The Text Publishing Company, Melbourne, Australia.

This edition published in 2009 by
House of Anansi Press Inc.
110 Spadina Avenue, Suite 801
Toronto, ON, M5V 2K4
Tel. 416-363-4343
Fax 416-363-1017
www.anansi.ca

Distributed in Canada by
HarperCollins Canada Ltd.
1995 Markham Road
Scarborough, ON M1B 5M8
Toll free tel. 1-800-387-0117

13 12 11 10 09   1 2 3 4 5

LIBRARY AND ARCHIVES CANADA CATALOGUING IN PUBLICATION

Garner, Helen, 1942–
The spare room / Helen Garner.
ISBN 978-0-88784-224-5
I. Title.

PR9619.3.G3S63 2009   823   C2008-906431-3

*We acknowledge for their financial support of our publishing program the
Canada Council for the Arts, the Ontario Arts Council, and the Government
of Canada through the Book Publishing Industry Development Program (BPIDP).*

Printed and bound in Canada

'It is a privilege to prepare the place
where someone else will sleep.'
ELIZABETH JOLLEY

1

FIRST, in my spare room, I swivelled the bed on to a north-south axis. Isn't that supposed to align the sleeper with the planet's positive energy flow, or something? She would think so. I made it up nicely with a fresh fitted sheet, the pale pink one, since she had a famous feel for colour, and pink is flattering even to skin that has turned yellowish.

Would she like a flat pillow or a bulky one? Was she allergic to feathers, or even, as a vegetarian, opposed to their use? I would offer choice. I rounded up all the extra pillows in the house, slid each one into a crisply ironed slip, and plumped them in a row across the head of the bed.

I pulled up the wooden venetian and threw open

the window. Air drifted in, smelling leafy, though you couldn't see a leaf unless you forced open the flywire screen and leaned right out. She had been staying for months with her niece Iris, on the eighth floor of an art deco apartment block in Elizabeth Bay whose windows, I imagined, pointed due north over a canopy of massive Sydney figs, towards the blue field of the harbour.

The immediate view from my spare room, until I could get some geraniums happening in a window box, was of the old grey paling fence that separated my place from my daughter Eva's. The sash window faced east, though, and the light bouncing off the weatherboard side of Eva's house kept the room bright till well into the afternoon. Also, it was late October, which in Melbourne is supposed to be spring.

I was worrying about her feet. The floor of her room was bare timber, except for a worn kilim full of rips. What if she snagged one of her long, elegant toes in it? What if she fell? Slippers were among the things she didn't bother with, along with suitcases, bras, deodorants, irons. I rolled up the dangerous kilim and threw it into the back shed. Then I drove over to a shop opposite Piedimonte's supermarket, where my friend Peggy, who knows about these things, said they sold tribal rugs. Straight away I spotted a pretty one: blossoms of watery green and salmon twining on a mushroom ground. The bloke told me it was Iranian, vegetable dyed. I chose it because it was faded. She would hate me to buy anything specially; to make a fuss.

Would she want to look at herself? It was months since I had last laid eyes on her: all I knew was from our emails. Every time the news sounded bad under her chirpy chatter, I would suggest flying up to Sydney. But she put me off. She was going out to dinner and couldn't change the date, or there wouldn't be a bed for me, or she didn't want me to waste my money. She might take it the wrong way if her room lacked a mirror. Behind the bookshelf in my workroom I found one I'd bought in an Asian import shop at Barkly Square and never used: a tall, narrow, unframed rectangle of glass, its back still equipped top and bottom with strips of double-sided adhesive tape. I selected a discreet spot for it, just inside the door of her room, and pressed it firmly against the plaster.

On the bedside table I fanned out some chord charts to have a crack at on our ukuleles—'Pretty Baby', 'Don't Fence Me In', 'King of the Road'. I arranged the reading lamp on a gracious angle, and placed beside it a mug full of nameless greenery that I'd found near the back shed. Then I went along the corridor to my room at the front of the house and lay on the bed with my boots on. It was four o'clock in the afternoon.

What woke me, ten minutes later, was a horrible two-stage smash, so sickening, so total, that I thought someone had thrown a brick through the side window. I rushed out all trembly and ran along the hall. Nothing moved. The house was quiet. I must have dreamt it. But the edge of the old hall runner, halfway to the kitchen, was weirdly sparkling. I stepped over it and into the spare room. The mirror no longer existed. The wall was bare, and the Iranian rug was thick with the glitter of broken glass.

I swept with the dustpan and brush, I beat with the millet broom, I hoovered in cunning angled strokes. The fragments of mirror were mean-shaped and stubborn, some so minuscule that they were only chips of light. They hid against the rug's scalp, in the roots of its fur. I got down on my knees and picked them out with my fingernails. When the daylight faded and I had to stop, my sister Connie rang me.

'A mirror broke? In her room?'

I was silent.

Then she said, in a low, urgent voice, 'Don't. Tell. Nicola.'

~

'Three weeks she's staying?' said my friend Leo, the psychiatrist. That Saturday evening I sat in the spartan kitchen of his South Yarra place and watched him cook. He poured the pasta into a strainer and flipped it up and down. 'Why so long?'

'She's booked in to do a course of alternative treatment down here. Some outfit in the city. They've fast-tracked her. She's supposed to present herself there first thing Monday morning.'

'What sort of treatment?'

'I was loath to ask. She talks about peroxide drips, awful stuff. She's already been getting big doses of vitamin C in Sydney. Eighty thousand units, she said. Intravenous. With something called glutathione. Whatever that is.'

He stood very still with the dripping colander in his hand. He seemed to be controlling himself: I had never before noticed the veins in his temples, under the curly white hair. 'It's bullshit, Helen.'

We started to eat. Leo let a shrink's silence fall, as he forked in food. His terrier, black and white, squatted by his chair and gazed up at him with helpless love.

'It is bullshit, is it?' I said. 'That's my instinct. Get this. When the bowel tumour showed up on the scan, she asked the oncologist to hold off treatment for a while. So she could take a lot of aloe vera. He said, "Nicola. If aloe vera could shrink tumours, every oncologist in the world would be prescribing it." But she believes in things. She's got one of those magnetic mats on the floor behind her couch. She says, "Lie on the mat, Hel. It'll heal your osteoporosis."'

Leo didn't laugh. He looked at me with his triangular brown eyes and said, 'And do you lie on it?'

'Sure. It's restful. She rents it from a shop.'

'So chemo didn't work.'

'She walked around carrying a bag of it plugged

into the back of her hand. She's had surgery. She had radiation. They've told her they can't do any more for her. It's in her bones, and her liver. They said to go home. She spent five days at a Petrea King workshop. I'd heard good things about that, but she said it wasn't her style. Then she went to someone she called a healer. He said she had to have her molars out—that the cancer was caused by heavy metals leaking out of her fillings.'

Leo put his head in his hands. I kept eating.

'Why is she coming to you?'

'She says I saved her life. She was about to send a lot of money to a biochemist up in the Hunter Valley.'

'A biochemist?'

'A kinesiologist told her this bloke's had a lot of success with cancer. So she phoned him up. He said he wouldn't need to see her. Just have a look at her blood picture. She was supposed to send him four grand and he'd post her the exact right herbs to target the cancers. "Essence of cabbage juice" was mentioned.'

I let out a high-pitched giggle. Leo looked at me steadily, without expression.

'And he told her she shouldn't worry if she heard unfavourable things about him, because he had enemies. People who were out to get him. I was trying to be tactful, so I asked her, "How did you feel, when he told you that?" She said, "I took it as a guarantee of integrity."'

My cheeks were hot. I knew I must be gabbling.

'I was scared she'd accuse me of crushing her last hope. So I went behind her back and called a journalist I know. He ran a check. Turns out the so-called biochemist's a well-known conman. He makes the most outlandish claims. Before he went into alternative health he'd spent years in gaol for armed robbery. I rang her just in time. She had the cheque book in her hand.'

It took me a moment to calm down. Leo waited. His kitchen was bare, and peaceful. I wondered if any of his patients had ever been invited into it. Outside the sliding glass doors an old concrete laundry trough sat on the paving, sprouting basil. The rest of the tiny yard was taken up by his car.

'You work with cancer patients,' I said. 'Does this sound bad?'

He shrugged. 'Pretty bad. Stage four.'

'How many stages are there?'

'Four.'

The bowl was empty. I put down my fork. 'What am I supposed to do?'

He put his hand on the dog's head and drew back its ears so that its eyes turned to high slits. 'Maybe that's why she's coming to stay. Maybe she wants you to be the one.'

'What one?'

'The one to tell her she's going to die.'

We listened to an old Chick Corea CD, and talked about our families and what we'd been reading. When it was late, he walked me to my car. The dog trotted at his heel. As I drove away up Punt Road I saw them dart across at the lights and plunge into the big dark gardens.

~

Rain fell in the night, quiet and kind. I woke at six with a sense of something looming, the same anxiety I felt before a writing deadline: the inescapable requirement to find something new in myself. Nicola would arrive today. I lay there under the shadow.

But I planted two new geraniums in a window box and hooked it on to the side fence outside her room. The bud-points, furled inside their leaves, reminded me of sharpened lead pencils. Their redness arrested my gaze before it hit the ugly palings.

Bessie came in from next door, squeezing through the gap in the fence while I was making a sandwich for lunch. She demonstrated a new hairclip application that kept her fringe still when she jumped up and down. Her nose was running and I kept wiping it on kitchen paper. The TV was on.

'Is that Saddam Hussein?' she said. 'What did he do, Nanna, to make him a baddie?'

I explained what a tyrant was. We began to philosophise. She pointed out that many people in the world were very poor. Then, tucking into the bowl of yoghurt and nuts that I placed before her, she observed that days differ from one another.

'Some are happy,' she said, 'but others are bad. I don't know why. Can I come to the airport with you? I want to tell Nicola I'm five-and-a-half. I think she'll be very surprised.'

~

We parked in plenty of time. The sun was out and the air was mild: we remarked gaily on the spring. As we marched hand in hand towards the Virgin Blue gate lounge, a crowd came surging out of it: Nicola's plane must have landed early. I broke into a trot, hauling Bessie behind me and scanning the approaching travellers for a tall, striding woman with prematurely white hair. We were almost on top of her before I recognised her. She was tottering along in the press of people, staggering like a crone, dwarfed by a confused young man who was carrying her Indian cloth bag over his shoulder. Bessie got a tighter grip on my hand.

'Hello darlings!' said Nicola. She was trying for insouciance, but her voice was hoarse, only a thread. 'This is my new friend Gavin. He's been so helpful!'

Gavin handed me the bag, murmured a farewell, and made for the exit. I took hold of Nicola's arm and steered her towards a row of hard chairs. She collapsed on to the first one. Bessie pressed closer to my other side, staring across me at Nicola with a look of fascinated panic.

'OK,' I said brightly. 'Let's sit here for a second and collect ourselves.'

But Nicola couldn't sit up straight. Her back was bowed right over, her neck straining as if under a heavy load. She was stripped of flesh, shuddering from head to foot like someone who has been out beyond the break too long in winter surf.

'Bessie,' I said. 'Listen to me, sweetheart. See that lady over there, behind the counter? Past the toilets? I want you to walk up to her and tell her we need a wheelchair. Right away. Will you be a big girl and do that?'

She stared at me. 'What if they don't have wheel-chairs at airports?'

'Bess. I need you to help us.'

Nicola turned on her a smile that would have once been beautiful and warm, but was now a rictus.

'But I don't want to go without you,' said Bessie on a high note.

'All right. You stay here with Nicola, and I'll go.'

'Nanna.' She gripped me with both hands.

'We have to get a wheelchair. Go to that lady and ask her. Otherwise I don't know how we'll get out of here.'

I pushed her away from me. She set out along

the carpeted hall with stiff, formal steps. I saw her rise on to her toes and try to show herself above the counter's edge. I saw the uniformed woman bend to hear her, glance up to follow her pointing finger, and turn to shout an order.

~

We got home to a house that still thought spring had come: all the windows up, the rooms flooded with mild, muggy air. Nicola hobbled down the hall on my arm while Bessie ran in front with her bag. We led her into the spare room and she sat shivering on the edge of the bed. I banged down the window and switched on the oil heater. No, thank you—she didn't want to drink, or eat, or wash, or go to the toilet. She was silent. Her head hung forward, as if a tiny fascinating scene were being enacted on her lap. I ran to the kitchen and put the kettle on for a hot water bottle. Bessie dawdled at the back door.

'Go home, sweetheart. I can't play with you now. Go home.'

She scowled at me and stumped off across the vegetable patch to the gap in the fence, where she hesitated, glaring at me over her shoulder, long enough for me to see her pearly skin, the vital lustre of her pouting lower lip.

In the spare room the oil was dripping and clicking inside the heater. I crouched in front of Nicola and pulled off her soft cloth shoes. Her bare feet were mottled, and icy to the touch; her ankles were laced with a pattern of blue veins. I hauled the jeans off her. She never wore knickers and she wasn't wearing any now. I opened the bag. The few garments she had stuffed into it—a wool spencer, a faded pink flannelette nightgown, a large hemp T-shirt—were grubby and neglected, full of holes, like the possessions of a refugee. *No one's looking after her. She's already lost.*

'Come on,' I said. 'Let's get this nightie on to you.' Like a child she raised both arms. I drew off her worn-out cashmere jumper and rag of a singlet. I thought I was keeping up a nonchalant pace, but when I saw the portacath bulging like an inverted bottle-top under the skin near her collarbone I must have missed a beat, for she began to whisper and croak: 'Sorry, Hel. Ghastly. So sorry.'

Uttering comforting, hopeful sounds, I fed each

of her arms into a sleeve and pulled the threadbare nightdress down to cover her. I got her under the doona. She couldn't find a position to lie in that didn't hurt.

When the two hot water bottles were ready I brought in a second doona, my thick winter one. I wrapped her, I swaddled her, I lay behind her spoon-wise and cuddled her in my arms. Shudders like electric shocks kept running down her body. Nothing could warm her.

But the heater gained command of the room. In a while she seemed to relax, and doze. I began to sweat. I eased back off the bed, turned the venetian blind to dark, and tiptoed out of the room.

How long had she been this bad? Why hadn't someone warned me? But who? She was a free woman, without husband or children. No one was in charge. I got a vegetable soup simmering in case she woke up hungry, and then I looked up her niece Iris in the Sydney phone book, and called her. A wheelchair? Oh no—this was *way* new. Could it have been just the strain of the flight? Oh God. We should absolutely stay in touch—here was her email address. Iris and her boyfriend Gab could come down, but not till the weekend after next—the school she was teaching at wouldn't give her any more time off. If it all turned out to be too much for me, they would take her home.

Too much for me? My pride was stung. I was supposed to be useful in a crisis.

Something rustled at the back door. Bessie slid into the kitchen, beaming, in a floor-length flounced skirt and fringed shawl.

'No, sweetheart—sorry. Not now.'

Her smile faded. 'But I've got a new dance to show you.'

'Nicola's asleep. She needs a very quiet house because she's terribly sick.'

She stared at me, sharply interested. 'Is Nicola going to die?'

'Probably.'

'Tonight?'

'No.'

She began to twist the doorknob, writhing and grizzling. 'I need you to play with me. I'm bored.'

'Don't push it, Bess. You heard what I said.'

'If you don't let me come in, I won't be able to stop whining.'

'Run home. Come back in the morning when she wakes up.'

'It's not even night-time yet!'

'She's asleep.'

'If you don't let me in, I'll whine more. I'll go berserk and do it even worse.'

I shoved back my chair. Its legs screeched on the boards and she bolted. Her flamenco heels went clicketing across the brick paving and she vanished behind the rocket bed.

I stopped on the back veranda. Further down the yard, beyond the shoulder-high broad beans with their black-and-white flowers, a small butternut pumpkin sat on the shed windowsill in what remained of the afternoon's sun. It had rested there, forgotten by both our houses, for months. If it hadn't dried out I could put it into the soup. I waited till I heard Bessie slam her back door, then I sneaked out and grabbed the pumpkin from the windowsill. It was suspiciously light. I stood it on the chopping board and pushed the point of the heavy knife through its faded yellow skin. Pouf. The blade sank through it. The pumpkin fell into two halves. The flesh was pale and fibrous, hardly more substantial than dust.

I hacked it into chunks and shoved them into the compost bin.

The night, when it came, was long. I woke many times. Once I heard the soft patter of rain. I parted the blind slats. A single light burned in the upper flat across the street: my comrade, that wakeful stranger. Towards four I crept along the hall and stood outside Nicola's closed door. Her breathing was slow and regular, but coarse and very loud.

I thought about the rattle that came out of my sister Madeleine's throat ten minutes before she died. 'Listen,' I said to her son who was sitting red-eyed by her bed with his elbows resting on his knees. 'She's rattling. She'll die soon.'

'Nah,' he said, 'it's just a bit of phlegm she's too weak to cough up.'

In the kitchen I switched on a lamp. There was a banana on the bench. Someone had started to peel it, eaten half, and lost interest. The rest of it lay abandoned in its loose, spotty skin.

2

THE BACK of my house faced south, but a triangular window had been set high into the roof peak, so that north light flooded into the kitchen. I was standing in a patch of sun when Nicola made her entrance. I looked up, ready to rush to her. Her hair was damp and flat against her skull. Her nightdress, dark with moisture, clung to her body. But her shoulders were back, her neck was upright, and she was smiling, smiling, smiling.

'Hello, darling!' she carolled, in her blue-blood accent. 'What a glorious morning! Oooh, there's that banana. I think I'll have it for breakfast. How did you sleep?'

My mouth hung open. 'How did you?'

'Oh, I was fine, once I dropped off. Actually I did perhaps sweat a bit. I'll run the sheets through your machine in a tick.'

She strolled in and established herself on a stool opposite me at the bench. Lord, she was a good-looking woman. She had the dignified cheekbones, the straight nose and the long, mobile upper lip of a patrician: the squatter's daughter that she was.

'My God, what a flight,' she said. 'I had a family with four kids behind me, and they fought all the way to Melbourne about who'd sit next to the mother.' She mimicked a high-pitched whine. 'I want to sit with you, Mummy. Look after *me*, Mummy. I don't love you any more, Mummy. I don't even like you. I hate you, Mum!'

She tossed her red wool shawl round her shoulders, raised her chin, and sparkled at me as if we were settling in at the Gin Palace for a martini and an hour's gossip.

'Now,' she said. 'Where's your phone? Professor Theodore told me to call him first thing.'

'Who's he?'

'He's the big cheese,' she said grandly. 'The whole thing's inspired by his theories. He's got to go overseas on Friday, though—that's why he made me come down a week early. He insists on seeing me this morning before I start the treatment.'

I passed her the cordless, went into the bathroom and closed the door. I could hear the tune, if not the words, of her telephone manner: innocently imperious, but sweetened by a confidential note, a bubbling stream of laughter. They'd be eating out of her hand. I turned on the shower.

When I emerged in my towel, she was sitting on the stool, holding the black handset in her lap. The flesh of her cheeks, what was left of it, had collapsed.

'He's already gone.'

'What?'

'To China. They said he left yesterday.'

A violent thrill ran down my arms and seethed in my fingertips. I closed my eyes. When I opened them, her smile was back in place.

'But it's all right. They said to come in anyway. A different doctor will see me. At four o'clock.'

'I'm coming with you.'

'Oh no, darling—I'll take the train. Just point me in the direction of the station.'

'You're not in any condition to walk to the station.'

'Of course I am! Look at me!' She spread her arms. The dark red shawl was draped becomingly this way and that.

'What about yesterday? I didn't know what to do. You could hardly put one foot in front of the other.'

'Oh, Hel! Did I give you a fright?' She gave a gusty laugh. 'You mustn't worry when I get the shivers. It's only a side-effect of the vitamin C driving out the toxins.'

'You mean you'd had the vitamin C yesterday? Before you went to the airport?'

She nodded, smiling hard, with her lips closed and her eyebrows high up into her forehead.

'Jesus, Nicola—is it always that brutal?'

'That was nothing. You should have seen me the first time. I had an afternoon appointment at a clinic on the North Shore. They pumped a bag of it into me. When they'd finished with me I was pretty shaken up. I needed to lie down for a while. But it was five o'clock and they were keen to close the rooms. They said to go home. I went out to the car but I knew

I couldn't drive. I could hardly even see. I felt so sick, all I could do was crawl into the back seat and lie down. I thought I'd stop shaking if I could get control of my breathing. But it kept getting worse. In the end I just got behind the wheel and drove home.'

'From the North Shore to Elizabeth Bay? At peak hour? You drove?'

She shrugged. 'Had to. Iris was a bit taken aback when I staggered in.'

She reached out for the remains of the banana, took a small bite and began to chew it carefully, with her front teeth and her incisors, right at the front of her mouth.

'Are your gums sore?'

'They've pulled out a couple of my molars.'

'Give us a look.'

She gulped down the scrap of banana and opened her jaws wide. I leaned across the bench on my elbows and peered in. Her tongue was quivering with the effort of lying flat. Halfway back, on either side, gaped a pink and pulpy hole. In the depths of each one I could see a lump of something white.

'Is that pus? Have you got an infection?'

'No, darling,' she said, wiping her lips on a tea

towel. 'It's just bone. The gum hasn't grown back over the gap. I can only chew with my front teeth, like a rabbit.' She laughed.

'But is it going to heal? Did they say it would?'

'Just watch me, babe. By the middle of next week, once the Theodore Institute's on the job, I'll have turned this whole damn thing around. The cancer will be on the run.'

Again the bright laugh, the twinkle, the eyebrows flying up towards the hairline. I couldn't meet her eye. I turned aside and looked out through the glass panels of the back door, into the yard. A streak of frilled fabric was darting along the path behind the broad beans. Oh no. Flamenco shoes rapped on the bricks, thundered on the veranda. The back door burst open.

'Here I am! Are you ready for my show?'

Nicola couldn't turn her head. She had to swing her whole body around. 'Who is this glorious señorita?'

Bessie leaned back from the hips and flung her arms in a high curve round her head. The blood-red nasturtium she had stuck into the elastic of her ponytail trembled there, its juicy stem already drooping. She bent her wrists and began to twine her hands round each other. Her fingernails were grimy, her palms padded with thick calluses from the school-yard monkey bars. She lowered her brow in a challenging scowl and paced towards us, flicking aside the bulk of her skirt with every step.

Nicola reared back on her stool. 'Stop. What's that cack on your lip?'

Bessie dropped her arms and ran the back of one hand under her nostrils. It left a glistening trail across her cheek.

'Oh shit.' Nicola got off the stool and backed away. 'I'm sorry, darling, but you can't come in here with a cold. I've got no resistance left. Helen, you'll have to send her home.' She shuffled as fast as she could down the hall into the spare room, and pulled the door shut behind her.

I picked up a pencil and took a breath to start explaining cell counts and immune systems, but Bessie didn't ask. She stood in the centre of the room with her arms dangling. Her face was blank. I heard the neighbour over the back lane slam his car door and drive away. At once his dog began its daily barking and howling. We had adapted our nerves to its tedious racket and no longer thought of complaining, but maybe the wind that morning was blowing from a new direction, for the high-pitched cries floated over the fence and right into our yard, filling the sunny air with lamentation.

~

Nicola wanted me to walk her to the station that afternoon and teach her the ticketing system so she could get to the clinic by herself each day, but it was her first consultation with these new people, and I'd heard it said that in such situations you needed a friend with you, someone less panicky than you and not deaf with fear, who could hear what the doctor said and remember it afterwards. I didn't mention any of this. I pressed her to let me drive her into the city, just this once, to show her the least confusing, the handsomest way to get there.

We parked under the Hyatt and strolled down Collins Street. The plane trees brushed their fresh leaves against the facades of the old-fashioned buildings. To Max Mara and Zambesi, Ermenegildo Zegna, Bang & Olufsen we paid no attention. She kept an eye out for juice shops and coffee bars. Umbrellas fluttered over the pavement tables. Big coaches from the country throbbed outside *The Lion King.* The chiming trams on Swanston Street excited her. I saw the beauty of my city and was proud that she saw it too.

We turned into the cool canyon of Flinders Lane. She snapped the rubber band off her bulging old Filofax and checked the number. 'This is it.'

The old building was tall and square and substantial, like the bank-shaped money-boxes we had as children, but its street frontage had been taken over by discount opal shops and fast food outlets: its white-tiled entryway was dilapidated, its grand mirrors speckled and scarred. As women in their sixties learn to do, we averted our eyes from our reflections, and made straight for the glass-fronted list of tenants: nine floors of people engaged in modest, honourable trades—button suppliers, bridal costumiers, milliners. The Theodore Institute: top floor. We peered through the lattice into the huge lift well with its swaying cables. Nicola pulled an apprehensive face. In the ancient cage as it clanked upward I felt too close to something fragile in her, something I could damage with my scepticism.

'This could be the Faraway Tree,' I said. 'I wonder what Land we'll find, at the top?'

She flashed me a tiny, grateful smile, and returned her gaze to the lino. I thought, I will kill anyone who hurts you. I will tear them limb from limb. I will make them wish they had never been born. *Almighty God*, I thought, *to whom all hearts are open.* The lift landed with a bump. It was four o'clock on the dot. The door slid open and we stepped out.

The hallway was dark and narrow. Each door had a panel of bathroom glass at eye level. One room was open: as we passed we glimpsed a girl with bowed head, sewing something under a cone of lamplight, while Tom Waits croaked away beside her on a radio.

We found the Theodore Institute at the very end of the hall. An empty wheelchair blocked the entry. The door was locked. We pressed the bell. No answer, though I sensed a vague commotion. I put my eye to the brass letter slot. Then a buzzer sounded beside us, and the door swung open. I stood back and Nicola led me in.

The room within was painted a strange yellow, the colour of controlled panic. Jonquils had dried in a vase on the reception counter, behind which a female attendant flustered at a computer. Several people sat on a row of folding chairs with their backs to a blank wall. One haggard woman, who had lost a leg, sat in silence with her hands clasped and her eyes down. Another was busy trying to thread a bright metallic scarf through the loops of a little black toque she wore on her bald head. I sat down while Nicola presented herself at the counter.

The toque woman caught my eye and smiled. 'I'm Marj. This is my husband Vin. We've come all the way from Broken Hill.' They both shook hands with me. Vin was a big, slow-moving bloke in shorts and tightly pulled up white socks. Marj went on tugging and pushing at the scarf.

'I like your hat,' I said. 'It's elegant.'

'Well,' she said with reckless gaiety, 'if you gotta go, you might as well go out sparkling.'

We all laughed, except the one-legged woman, who had not raised her eyes from the remainder of her lap. Meanwhile I could hear the attendant, a plain, brown-haired girl with a high ponytail who had introduced herself as Colette, chattering away to Nicola at the counter.

'I know it's a disappointment for you, but Professor Theodore suddenly had to go to China! And he won't be back till next week. Don't you worry, though, because we've got another doctor. He usually only comes in on Fridays to make a presentation, but this week he'll be here on a Monday. And he'll see you!'

I could see Nicola nodding and nodding, propping herself on the counter with trembling forearms.

'What's Professor Theodore actually doing, in China?' I called out from my metal chair. 'Because he did make a special point of wanting to examine Nicola before she started the program. Couldn't he have let her know his plans had changed?'

I was trying to sound courteous and firm, but the vibe in the room stiffened and an uncomfortable silence fell.

Colette's voice dropped an octave. 'Oh,' she murmured, 'it's a very important international conference.' Her face radiated a timid solemnity. She spread her palms and lifted her shoulders and eyebrows: the obligations of this demi-god, her employer, were beyond her ken. No one looked at me. Nicola, credit card in hand, kept her back to me. I subsided, but my heart was thumping.

By the time Nicola had filled in a thick form and forked out two thousand dollars for the opening week's program, it was after five o'clock. 'You'll be seen in half an hour!' cried Colette. We settled down to wait. In rooms beyond the reception area we sensed movement, heard voices. Once or twice a chubby man with a buzz-cut popped his head round the door and bestowed a benign smile on the people numbly waiting. Were we imagining it, or did the air of the clinic smell faintly pleasant? An elusive odour from nature, or even from our distant childhoods? Was it the scent of summer? We could not pin it down.

Nicola folded her long legs under her in yoga position on her chair, and opened an Alexander McCall-Smith novel she had had the sense to bring. I flipped in silence through ragged back numbers of *New Weekly*, looking for cosmetic surgery disasters to sneer at. Once we would have gone into paroxysms together at a condition called *trout mouth*. Now, angry and full of fear, I kept it to myself.

There was a water filter in a corner, and a tower of plastic cups, but nothing to eat. It had not occurred to us to bring food. Marj and Vin shared a sandwich wrapped in foil. At six I took the lift down to the street. In the low sun, city workers were still streaming along Swanston Street towards the station. I bought two bottles of fruit juice in a sandwich bar.

When I rushed back in, the atmosphere of humble patience had not wavered. I thrust a bottle into Nicola's hand and she guzzled its contents.

At half past six Marj from Broken Hill shifted in her seat, leaned forward and began to cough. A hacking and a rending convulsed her; a tearing intake of breath followed each spasm. She discreetly spat the proceeds into a tissue and stowed it in a plastic bag. No one spoke. We had now been waiting for almost three hours.

Just before seven, Colette burst out from an inner room and made a joyful announcement. 'Hello, everyone! At seven o'clock we're going to have a presentation. And after that, Nicola, Dr Tuckey will see you.'

At last Tuckey wandered into the reception area. We raised our weary eyes to him. His face, floating on the sea of himself, was oddly disarming.

'Half the staff are away this week,' he murmured, 'so we're in a bit of chaos.'

I raised my hand. 'Can you tell us what effect on

the week's arrangements the absence of Professor Theodore is likely to have?'

The other patients turned their heads listlessly, then withdrew eye contact.

The doctor looked right at me, but he seemed almost shy. 'You mean on the, uhm, quality of the treatment?' he said.

'No,' I said, 'I mean will things be better organised than they've been today? Because we need to know how to arrange our time. So I can deliver my friend here every morning and pick her up every afternoon. And keep our lives outside of here running in some sort of reasonable way.'

Vin from Broken Hill flicked me a look, along which travelled what I read as a tiny current of solidarity. He didn't believe in this rigmarole either. He had to pretend to because his wife was desperate, because he loved her. Tuckey murmured something reassuring, still far short of an apology. Again my heart was thudding. My cheeks were red. Nicola looked at me kindly, then away again. I felt I had shamed her. I held my tongue.

The doctor set up a screen against a wall, opened a laptop on the counter, and stood resting one elbow beside it. Without having to be asked, we shuffled our chairs into better viewing positions. Somebody sighed. He pressed the first key and up came the title of his talk: 'Cancer and It's Treatments'. I didn't dare look at Nicola: not because she would laugh, but because I was afraid she wouldn't.

'I'm going to tell you,' Dr Tuckey began, 'about our key cancer-killing therapies. You know how an octopus can break a big rock with its tentacles? Well that's what a cancer cell's like.'

Did he mean the cell was like the octopus or like the rock? The doctor's manner, as he worked his way down the dot points, was modest and amiable, almost soothing. Everything about him was spongy, without defence: you could not hate him. But his discourse had a stupefying effect. My mind veered about, seeking something to grip. I was tired, I was hungry. My concentration waxed and waned. Once or twice I nodded off. This was not the moment to zone out. I pushed my chair back a few feet and sneaked the notebook and pen out of my bag.

'Stress,' he said, 'is the biggest cause of cancer in our society. Stress makes us vulnerable to whatever nasties we have lurking in our beings.'

That wasn't so outlandish. My thoughts coasted sideways to my sister Madeleine, her relentless grief and rage when her husband drowned in the surf: how she wielded without mercy the manipulative power of her suffering. Ten years later an untreatable cancer was found in her lung. She accepted her death sentence quietly, without mutiny; perhaps, we thought in awe, she even welcomed it. She laid down her gun. She let us cherish her. We nursed her. In less than a year, with her family near her, she put aside her knitting and died, in her own house, in the bed she had shared with her husband, while outside the window the shapely limbs of the trees they had planted together stood leafless in the late winter air.

'If people are struck by lightning and survive,' the doctor was saying, 'their cancers shrink and disappear.'

I glanced at the other listeners. No one seemed to find this strange.

'A fissure in the earth under your house can disturb the electro-magnetic field. In Germany, quite a high percentage of cancer victims are living over one of these.'

A fissure? Didn't I read about that in the seventies? People whose living room floor collapsed into a disused mine shaft? Whose grand piano slid into the chasm and vanished forever? And on top of that they got cancer?

Nicola's head was cocked in a posture of intent listening.

'The incidence of certain sorts of cancer is known to be much lower round the equator. This is good, solid research—published just a few months ago.'

Now I was wide awake.

'High dosage vitamin C will kill off lumps of cancer and boost the immune system. And our ozone sauna treatment is based on the old natural-therapy approach to cancer—sweating out the toxins. Most doctors don't know this stuff. But it's good science.'

Nicola sat chin in hand, her handsome face suffused with an expression of deep pleasantness, offering the doctor generous eye contact, and nodding, always nodding.

Vin from Broken Hill laid his hand on his wife's legs, which were now resting across his lap. His tenderness moved something painful in me. It rebuked me in my suspicion and contempt. What did I know about cancer? Maybe there was something in these cockamamie theories. Maybe they were the future. Maybe Leo was wrong when he stated that vitamin C did not shrink tumours. Maybe it *was* unfair that these pioneers had fallen foul of the authorities and were obliged to treat their patients in shabby private clinics.

But I couldn't help sneaking looks at the loose swag of flesh that overlapped the waistband of Dr Tuckey's trousers. His shirt buttons divided it into a double burden. It did not appear to be meaningfully attached to his frame. It swayed half a beat behind his movements: it trembled, it hung, a shapeless cargo of meat.

~

At a quarter past eight that first evening, four hours after the time of her appointment, Nicola was called in to see Dr Tuckey.

'Come on, Hel,' she said, stowing the novel into her shoulder bag and setting out for the inner room. I paused at the door but Nicola did not hesitate. She barged in and took the first chair she saw. I scurried after her.

A cold fluoro strip lit a scene of disorder, as of recent arrival or imminent flight. The whole floor was taken up by cardboard cartons, some of them in toppling waist-high stacks, others split and spewing manila folders. Empty metal shelves stood about on pointless angles. The window was unshielded except for a broken venetian that hung derelict on one cord.

The surface of the desk across which the doctor greeted us with a genial nod was strewn with electronic cables. He shoved aside a large TV monitor and made a narrow space for Nicola's file, which he began to open and close with penguin-like flappings of his hands. She launched a coherent account of her cancer, the discovery of it in her bowel, her theories about its origins, the history of its progress through her body, and the array of treatments she had already undergone. Dr Tuckey listened with flowing gestures of comfort and sympathy, like an old lady hovering over the tea things: frowning and clicking his tongue and shaking his head and raising his eyebrows and pursing his lips. Then, when Nicola fell silent, he began to speak.

'You sound like the perfect person,' he said, 'for our kind of approach.'

She straightened her spine and leaned back in her chair. She was smiling.

'Yes,' he said. 'I think you'll respond to it very well.'

~

That night Nicola wet the bed. I came upon her in the hall at two o'clock, backing out of the spare room with an armful of sheets. 'I had a dream,' she said, 'and when I woke up in the middle of it I had piss running out of me. I made it to the toilet for the rest of the stream, but look. I've made a mess.'

This was the closest I had ever seen her to embarrassment. We were old bohemians, long past shame at basic bodily functions.

'Give me those,' I said. 'I stocked up on manchester before you came.'

'Manchester? This is like an Elizabeth Jolley novel.'

We started to laugh. She sat on the chair while I made up her bed afresh. I saw her bare feet on the rug and thought of my mother, how she would clean up after me when as a child I had what she called 'a bilious attack'. I remembered her patience in the middle of the night, the precious moments of her attention, in the house full of sleeping children who had usurped my place in her affections. In a trance of gratitude I would watch her spread the clean sheet across my bed, stretch it flat and tuck in its corners, making it nice again for the disgusting, squalid creature I had become. Without revulsion, she would pick up my soiled sheets in her arms and bear them away.

3

ON TUESDAY morning we took the train to the city. I showed her how to avoid the chaos of Flinders Street Station by getting off at Parliament; we walked down to the Theodore Institute together. Sensing wariness in Colette's greeting, I left Nicola there to settle in for her first treatment, and went downstairs to get myself a coffee.

Twenty minutes later, when I returned, the waiting room was empty. No one seemed to be in charge. I ran my eye over the framed diplomas on the wall behind the reception desk. Ah, here were Tuckey's credentials: a lot of polysyllabic alternative stuff with curlicues, and a string of initials that looked medical. All right, but where the hell was he? Who was running this joint?

I could hear Colette behind a partition, gaily bashing someone's ear about her passion for figure skating. There was a bell on the counter. I rang it. She popped her head in and directed me to a side door.

Beyond it, in a cramped space whose window, if you stood on your toes, gave a side view of the cathedral, I found Nicola enclosed to the chin in a sort of low tent; her grinning face poked out at the top through a hole that was sealed round her neck with a strip of plastic and a pink towel. The strange perfume from nature that we had remarked upon the day before hung in the air again.

'What the hell is this? You look like a cartoon lady in a weight-loss clinic.' Again we laughed.

'It's an ozone sauna. Look inside.'

I unzipped the front of the tent and saw her seated on a white plastic chair, naked but for a towel, and holding in each hand a wand-like object wrapped in kitchen paper. The perfumed vapour oozed out in wisps. I closed the zip. She tilted her head towards a murky sheet of A4 paper pinned to the wall. I stepped up to look. It was a list of instructions on resuscitation. We regarded each other without expression.

'What are those things you're holding?'

'Electrodes.' She shut her eyes and leaned back.

Electrodes. I held my peace. Morning sunshine fell into the room through the high window. The ozone smelled delicious, very subtle and refreshing, like watermelon, or an ocean breeze. I sat on a chair in the corner and pulled the lid off my coffee.

~

An hour later, Colette bustled in and ushered Nicola to another room. There she lay on her back on a high, hard bed that was covered with flowered cloth, while the young woman applied Chinese cups to her shoulder, her neck and her belly. Like many people I knew, I had submitted to cupping once or twice, and thought nothing of it either way; but these cups had nipples with tubes running into them, through which more ozone was to be pumped from a large, rusty-looking tank attached to the wall by a metal chain around its girth.

It seemed an intimate procedure and I kept offering to leave, but both Nicola and Colette urged me to stay. I pressed myself into a corner and folded my arms. The east-facing window gave on to an attractive jumble of spires and domes, and beyond them a sky packed with woolly spring clouds.

'What does the ozone do, Colette?' asked Nicola pleasantly.

Colette, finished with the cups, was riffling through a file with her back to Nicola. Without turning around she replied in a distracted tone, 'Kills cancer.'

'Oh. Right.'

'And the vitamin C,' continued Colette, laying down the file and turning to make fierce clawing motions with both hands, 'sort of scoops the cancer cells out of your body.'

Once more, still smiling, Nicola let her eyelids droop. With a merry wave and a pert flip of her ponytail, Colette left the room. I drifted over to the bench under the window, where she had left Nicola's file. Casually I slid the papers out of the manila folder. I turned a page and the heading *Prognosis* leapt at me. Under it someone had written, in a sprawling, immature hand, 'Terminal, 1–3 years.'

I dropped the sheet and leaned towards the window. Out there, on the west side of the cathedral, someone had carved gargoyles, and a couple of saintly men with staffs and stone haloes. My legs were quivering. I took a few deep breaths. What was going on? Hadn't Dr Tuckey, the night before, assured Nicola that she would 'respond very well' to the clinic's treatment? Surely he should have said, 'Would you like me to tell you what I think your future is?' And if she said yes, wouldn't it have been more honourable to tell her the truth, and then say, 'But we can offer you certain treatments that may shrink the cancer, slow it down, make it possible for you to live more comfortably in the time you have left'?

Maybe he couldn't do it while I was in the room. Maybe he didn't have the authority, within their outfit, to speak about death. Maybe only Professor Theodore, the guru, had that power.

Behind me on her high bed, Nicola's eyes were still closed. I tidied the sheets of paper into the folder and lined it up with the edge of the bench.

She spoke. 'Helen. Would your sister Madeleine have come to a place like this?'

'Not in a fit.'

'Not even if she'd known about it?'

'No way. She wouldn't have contemplated it for a single second.'

'Why?'

Because she'd have seen immediately that it was a con. I couldn't say that. I didn't have the knowledge to make a judgment. And if I did condemn it, where could Nicola turn? What would be left? Drop all weapons and face death? Who was I to tell her she had to do that?

So I said, 'Madeleine had been a nurse. Her husband was a surgeon. Her whole life was lived in the world of western medicine. She believed in it. Those were the terms and language she thought in.'

She lay quiet for a while, with the cups bulging on her belly like a row of breasts. Then she opened her eyes and gazed towards the window.

'I'm expecting an angel to drop out of those clouds at any minute,' she said, and turned on me her cheekiest, most challenging smile.

~

After lunch, which we imbibed in the form of large vegetable juices in a cafe, Colette dropped heavy hints that I should leave: apparently they were about to beam some kind of light on to her. I gathered up my things and made off. I went to David Jones' food hall and bought a couple of flathead fillets for our dinner, then wandered round the city, priding myself on not squandering money. When I called for Nicola later in the afternoon, she was in good spirits.

At home I went out the back to unpeg the dry sheets from the clothesline. She insisted on helping me. I could see it cost her something to raise her arms to shoulder height, but together we folded the bed linen perfectly and laid it in the cupboard. Then, following her instructions, I made the sort of fish soup with vegetables that a semi-vegetarian could eat. She ate with appetite, and even drank a glass of dry sherry. We watched the news and dissected with cheerful meanness the latest escapades of her old friend my ex-husband.

'Tomorrow,' she said at bedtime, as I handed her the hot water bottle wrapped in a clean tea towel, 'they're giving me some more vitamin C.'

I looked up. 'Want me to come with you?'

She shrugged. 'Bring a book.'

I heard her moving about not long after midnight, and came out to check. Her shoulder and neck were hurting. Again she was wet, but not with piss. It was sweat: the bed-clothes were soaked, almost through to the mattress, and even the pillow was sodden. Three times that night I tackled the bed: stripped and changed, stripped and changed. This was the part I liked, straightforward tasks of love and order that I could perform with ease. We didn't bother to put ourselves through hoops of apology and pardon. She sat limply on the chair and watched me work.

'I should have been a nurse,' I said. 'Like my sisters.'

She gave a faint laugh. 'Matron. With a rustling veil.'

'Or maybe a detective. Why didn't I join the police force in the seventies, instead of trying to be a bloody hippie? Which I was never any good at.'

'You can be quite fierce. But they would have made mincemeat of you.'

'What painkillers have you got, Nicola?'

'Digesic.'

'Is that all?'

'I can have eight a day. I'll take some now.'

I went for the glass of water and stood at the bed while she gulped down the pills.

'What does *gesic* mean?' I said.

'Must be Greek.'

'Must be. Rectogesic is for piles. Analgesic...'

'*Anal*-gesic,' she said, 'should be for sore bums.'

'Ha ha! And *Di*-gesic'—it came thundering down on us like a truck: no time to jump out of its way—'is so you won't *die.*'

She laughed, closed her eyes, and lay back on the clean pillow.

Just before daybreak, as I lay sleepless in my bed, a weird little storm exploded right overhead, dumped twenty drops of rain, and fled onwards at a clip. The street was quiet. The air was fresh and cool. Something tiptoed across the leaf mulch outside my open window and paused there, breathing, to groom itself.

4

AT BREAKFAST time Nicola was in pain. Her shoulders were bent. It was hard for her to walk.

'Shouldn't we get you some stronger drugs?' I said.

'Don't worry,' she said. 'It's the treatments causing the pain—that's how I know they're working. It's just the toxins coming out.'

She chewed a morsel of toast with honey and drank a cup of tea.

I took her into the city.

This time an unsmiling middle-aged stranger with an Eastern European accent was on duty in the treatment room. His white coat and slow, almost tranquillised movements lent him an air of authority lacking in the endearing but twitty Colette. He did not bother to introduce himself, but told Nicola to lie on her back on the high bed, hooked a bag of clear fluid on to a tall metal stand, and prepared to plug a tube into the portacath on her chest. Nicola held up one hand.

'The last nurse who gave this to me,' she said, her voice high with tension and posher than usual, 'did it too fast. It hurt me and I was awfully sick and weak afterwards. Can I ask you, please, to make sure it's not going to run too fast?'

The man in the white coat paused in his manipulation of the equipment. 'I'm not a nurse,' he said. 'I'm a specialist.'

I got off my chair and stepped forward. 'Excuse me,' I said. I cleared my throat. 'Excuse me, doctor, but my friend's had violent reactions to the vitamin C. Are you sure it's appropriate?'

The man didn't look at me. He stood quite still with the tube in his hand. 'It's written here,' he said, 'that your friend is to have vitamin C today. And that's what I will give her.'

I moved further in so that my shoulder was beside Nicola's and the man had to meet my eye. He gave me a long, measuring stare. I took a breath, but Nicola put her hand on my arm.

'It's all right, Hel. I just got a bit panicky for a second.'

I felt her shoulder relax: all those years of yoga. She bathed the man in her patrician smile.

'I trust you, doctor,' she said. 'I'm sure you know exactly what you're doing. Carry on.'

Carry on? The wind went out of my sails. I returned to my chair. The needle pierced the ring of stretched skin, the liquid began to swell and drip in its tube, and the man left the cubicle with his slow tread.

'Did I take the wrong tone to him?' whispered Nicola. 'What did I do?'

'He's a fucking prick, that's what's wrong. He's got a thing about your accent, and he probably thinks we're dykes.'

'I thought you were going to thump him. You've gone all red.' She looked at me reproachfully. She even started to giggle.

'He shouldn't talk to you like that.' I got out the lipstick and stabbed at my mouth.

'Don't hang around, Hel. Go home and do some

work. I'll text you when I'm finished.'

I didn't have any work: I had cancelled everything I could for her stay. But I ran down the nine flights of tiled stairs and tramped off to Flinders Street.

I wasn't used to taking the Broadmeadows train at mid-morning. It was empty and rather calming, forging along the river, past the Docklands stadium and out through North Melbourne. It racketed across the dry creek bed; it slid between the old warehouses and ran parallel with the steel-buttressed brick wall that held Bellair Street back from the railway line. I never quite trusted that wall not to collapse on to the tracks; yet there it stood, fifteen feet high and bulging but still stable, accepting the morning sun on its pocked and rosy surfaces. Something softened in my chest and I took the first proper breath of the day. All right. Let this ludicrous treatment be what it is. Go home and put your house in order.

Nicola's bedclothes were still askew from the night's turmoil. I pulled off the damp sheets, then hauled the mattress off its base and leaned it against the open door to air in the sun. I was in the backyard pegging out the first load of washing when Eva sang out to me from her garden. I headed through the bean rows to the gap in the fence but she called in a croak, 'Don't come near me. We're all down with stinking colds.'

'What—even Mitch?' Her husband was famous for never, ever getting sick.

'All of us. It's going round Hughie's creche. I've been keeping the kids away from your house. Bessie misses you. She's sitting in front of the TV gushing tears. We're running out of food.'

Stoical Eva stood barefoot in her nightie beside the guinea pigs' hutch. Hughie drooped on her shoulder. He lifted his face from the tangled mass of her hair. His gaze was dull. Poor kids.

I drove, I bought, I paid. I delivered to Eva's doorstep cardboard cartons overflowing with organic foodstuffs. She wouldn't even open the screen door till I had closed their front gate behind me.

In my kitchen, dishes soon dripped in their wire rack. The bench-tops shone. Clean linen lay folded in sweet-smelling piles. I took a brief nap to prepare myself for another night of disturbance and lamp-lit labour. Then I lined up the ingredients for a dainty soup of dashi, tofu and noodles. How competent I was! I would get a reputation for competence.

Nicola called me at five and announced in her grandest voice that the day's treatments were done. She brushed aside my offers: she was about to take a taxi home. I arranged myself on the sofa facing the door, and waited for her.

Towards six o'clock a key was laboriously inserted into the front door, and a silhouette came shuffling down the hall. Her shoulders were bowed, her knees were sagging; her head was thrust forward on a neck that was almost horizontal. Oh, what had they done to her? I jumped to my feet. But as she came into the light of the kitchen I saw on her face again that terrible smile, the grimace that said, *Do not ask me any questions.*

'Not crash hot,' she mumbled, gripping the corner of the bench with both hands. 'Straight to bed.'

'Will I bring you something to eat, in a minute? A thimbleful of soup? On a tray?'

She shook her head. Every bit of visible skin bore a sheen of sweat, but she kept that smile screwed on, her eyebrows pushed high into her forehead. She turned and hobbled back along the hall to her room. I heard the window slam.

I boiled the kettle and wrapped the hot water bottle in its cloth. Her door was shut. Was I supposed to knock? I opened it and slid in. She was lying on her back on the bed, fully dressed, with her eyes closed. The late sun glared in off the wall next door, making the room comfortless and harsh.

'What's that smell?' she said, without opening her eyes. 'Is it me?'

'I can't smell anything.' I laid the hot water bottle against her side.

'Smells funny. Yuk.'

I sniffed. With the window shut there was a smell, like a woollen jumper in the rain. I got down on my knees and took a whiff of the new Iranian rug.

'It must be the dye in the carpet. Will I take it out?'

She didn't answer. I rolled it up and hauled it out into the corridor. Then I pulled the cord of the venetian blind and the room went dim. Still she said nothing. Her breathing was speeding up. She took a gasp of air and her teeth began to chatter.

'Nicola. What do you need me to do?'

'Sleep. I wanna sleep. Go out. Thanks.'

I longed to slip her shoes off, to draw a cotton

blanket over her. But I was scared to touch her. I was afraid of her weakness, afraid of her will. So I stepped out of the room and closed the door behind me.

~

There was sweat in the night. There was pain in belly and shoulder. Each time I heard her moving about I would enter her room, without speaking. She tried to smile at me: she was pretending not to suffer. All she had to help her was the last of the day's Digesic. I brought water in the china jug with the pink hydrangea pattern, and poured it into my prettiest glasses: I drank too, to keep her company. The intravenous vitamin C seemed to brutalise her spine: she could not hold herself erect. I nursed her, stripping and bundling, breaking out new linen, refreshing her bed and refreshing it again. While I worked she sat in the corner on the wooden chair, with her head hanging forward and her long, bruised hands clasped in her lap.

At last she fell into a proper sleep. I crawled back into my bed, and the house was still.

~

In the morning, stupid with fatigue, I was preparing breakfast when she walked into the kitchen. She moved very slowly, but her head was up. The glazed smile was back in place. She sat on a stool, accepted a dish of yoghurt and fruit, and spooned it up in tiny quantities.

'Listen,' I said. 'Have you told the people at the clinic you're in pain?'

She looked up, surprised. 'Oh, darling,' she said, sounding almost bored. 'They treat cancer. Pain's a given. They're not interested in my pain.'

I turned away to the sink and yanked on the rubber gloves.

'Sorry about last night,' she went on airily. 'It's the vitamin C. That's what the pain is—the cancer being wrenched out of me.'

I kept my back to her and tipped the cutlery into the dishwater.

'Still,' I said. 'You need more sleep than you're getting. I'm wondering if you should see a GP—get a script for something a bit stronger than the Digesic?'

She laid down her spoon. 'Helen,' she said. 'I have to trust the vitamin C. By the middle of next week it'll have the damn thing on the run. I need you to believe in it too.'

Till this minute I had dodged the question by concentrating on simple tasks. Now I took my first real breath of it, the sick air of falsehood. I forced myself to nod. I lowered my eyes and scrubbed at the prongs of a fork. OK. It was Thursday. She copped the intravenous vitamins only on alternate days: this morning she'd have the more benevolent bullshit, the ozone and the cupping. But Friday night would be another horror stretch. I would have to get cunning.

~

I dropped her at the Theodore Institute, then drove in a big arc along the river and out to Leo's place. Maybe I could catch him between patients. I rattled the knocker. The dog's nails skittered on the floorboards. Leo opened the door and looked at me in surprise. He glanced crossly at his watch, and at the gate behind me.

'I'll be quick. It's about Digesic.'

'Is that all she's got?' He took a long, slow breath. 'Bad nights?'

I nodded. A frantic lump rose in my throat. I gulped it down. 'What'll I do?'

'That won't be strong enough now. Eight a day's the upper limit. Panadeine Forte might be better. Or morphine. But a GP won't give an unknown patient morphine. Get on to her oncologist in Sydney. He can fax an authorisation down. And don't hesitate to ask. Oncologists expect that sort of thing.'

'Is it ethical for me to do that?'

'She's putting a lot of pressure on you. It's perfectly kosher for you to get help.'

The gate latch clinked and a woman in a business suit and heels came up the path. I stood back. Leo smiled at her, and gestured gracefully towards the open door. She kept her eyes away from mine as she passed me. Her discretion was exemplary but it irritated me. I felt like shouting at her, 'I am not a patient!' She stepped across the threshold and disappeared down the hall. I turned to leave.

Leo put his hand on my shoulder. 'Helen. You can't be useful if you're scared shitless. If you want to play hardball, why don't you get in touch with the palliative people? They come to your house. I know it sounds drastic, but tomorrow's Friday. Weekends can be scary unless you've got back-up.'

I ran to my car. Where did he keep the dog while he worked? Did it have a beanbag in the kitchen to sleep on, a bone to gnaw, a flat bowl of fresh water? Was it happy? Were dogs supposed to be happy? Maybe the belief in the responsibility to be happy was the dumbest idea anyone ever had.

~

Nicola came home that day all soothed and heartened. I didn't mention pain and neither did she. She rested a while in her room, then we watched the TV news, and ate our dinner on the veranda. Against the shed wall the broad beans stood in their hopeful rows, a gratifying green. The sky flushed and turned dusky. The coloured lorikeets darting in and out of next door's palm tree reminded us of the kookaburra that had swooped one day on her lunch table, snatched in its beak a fist-sized slab of expensive Danish butter, and soared away to a high branch: later we spotted the greedy bird standing in the undergrowth near the tank, leaning forward with its beak agape like a drunk outside a pub.

'I wish I'd brought my uke,' she said, wiping away the tears of laughter. 'I don't even remember the last time we had a play.'

'How long since you've been home?'

'Oh, months. I had to stay at Iris's, to be near St Vincent's for the radiation. And anyway I haven't got the muscle to drag myself up the hill.'

Nicola lived beyond the northern beaches of Sydney on a hillside that could be reached only by boat. For years she had chugged back and forth in a tinnie between Palm Beach jetty and the landing below her house, a ten-minute ride in fine weather. She would collect me from my car on the Palm Beach side, urge me down the white wooden ladder with the groceries, and make the outboard roar with one yank of the cord. Away we bounced. She sat at the tiller, erect and handsome as a duchess in loose garments that the wind ballooned and rippled, her silver hair streaming flat against her skull.

Under her practical and good-humoured command, skimming across the water and hauling the bags up the steep bush track to the house, I was safe. On her territory I deferred to her and obeyed her. She knew about ticks and leeches, snakes, goannas;

the names of birds and their habits; the movements of the moon; how to save water; how to manage an outdoor fire. She was older, taller, braver, and more free: she had taught herself to live alone.

The first time I went to stay a weekend, she dared me to climb the bush-choked escarpment that soared up behind her shack to Kuringai Chase. We clawed our way to the top, grunting and cursing, and hauled ourselves, two filthy, panting hags, out of the scrub on to a track along which at that moment came strolling a city couple in pale, freshly ironed sporting clothes, with a Shih-tzu trotting on a leash. All afternoon we lay on our beds and read mighty works of literature, shouting to each other analytical or admiring remarks.

That night we took the bottle of Stoly down the rough path to the landing where, sitting on our jackets in the dark, we launched the long conversation that would become our friendship. She told me about the only man she had ever lived with, Hamish, whose children she loved and was still in touch with, but who had been a brute to her; and an Aboriginal bloke who, in the days when she was doing a lot of acid and having a sort of crack-up in a rainforest, had wandered in from nowhere and saved her from starving herself to death.

When she was about seven, she said, a neighbour in his twenties had come over the fence one afternoon while she was playing in the yard. 'He ran away. I picked myself up and hid at the top of the back steps. I stayed out there till it got dark and I could hear my mother and my sister calling me. I knew I could never, ever tell anyone what had happened. And I never did.'

I was already half drunk. I said, 'Fuckin' animal. Is he still alive?'

She shrugged.

'Don't you want to hunt him down and bash the shit out of him? I'll help you. We can look in the electoral rolls.'

She uttered a laugh of good-natured scorn. We hunched on the end of the old timber wharf. Masts were jingling. On the black, restless water of the inlet, boats' riding lamps were laying down what she said a poet had called *stacked saucers of light*.

Now, on my back veranda, she said, 'I want to go home as soon as I finish at the Theodore. I can't wait to. But I've been too weak to pull the starter cord on the outboard.'

'Couldn't you get one of those self-starters? Where you just have to press a button?'

'They only make them for thirty horsepower or more. If I had thirty in my tinnie it'd be vertical.'

We sat on the bench doubled over. Oh, I loved her for the way she made me laugh. She was the least self-important person I knew, the kindest, the least bitchy. I couldn't imagine the world without her. She would not admit it, but her house was unreachable now. Unless someone carried her there on his back, she would never go home again.

With our feet among the empty plates we talked about movies we might go to next week, once she had settled into the routine of the treatments; and we pretended not to hear the exiled Bessie bouncing on the trampoline behind the wisteria hedge, singing a melancholy song interspersed with bouts of juicy coughing.

5

WE WENT to bed early. I slept in jerky, shallow bouts, and dreamed confused tales of failure and frustration. When I woke at six and walked into the kitchen to raise the blinds I almost tripped over her: she was crouching on the floor with her arms round her knees, making tiny rocking movements. Her bed, when I went to look, was a twisted mess of wet sheets.

'I didn't want to wake you,' she said. 'God, I'm so sick of this pain.'

Together, not speaking, just working, we got her up and washed and dried and on to the couch. I threw open the windows and tucked a rug around her. Her face was white.

'Can you tell me where it hurts?'

'Here. Neck. Shoulder. I must have pulled a muscle turning over in bed.'

'What did you take, in the night?'

'Digesic. I only had two left. I've run out.'

'Right. Today we're getting you some proper painkillers.'

With difficulty she raised her knees. 'The hospital in Sydney did give me a script for slow-release morphine.'

'Great. I'll take it to the chemist while you're at the clinic.'

'Yeah but Hel—I left it at Iris's.' She glanced at me with a crooked smile.

I couldn't seem to close my mouth. I swallowed. 'I'll email her today, then, and get her to post it down.'

She stiffened. 'How did you get her email? I don't want you two hassling each other.'

'What? Well, call your oncologist in Sydney. Get her to set up a source of morphine down here.'

She clicked her tongue. 'Oh no, darling—I couldn't call her. Anyway she won't be there. She teaches at the university three days a week.'

'Nicola. They have telephones at universities.'

'No, I can't bother her.'

'Bother her?' My voice shot up the scale. 'You're her patient. It's her job, it's her duty, to stop you from being in pain.'

She rolled her head on the cushion and looked out the window. I stood waiting at the bench with the dishcloth in my hand. And with a flick of her patrician manner she changed the subject.

'You won't need to drive me into town today, thanks, Helen,' she said. 'I'll take the train.'

I wrung out the cloth with a violent twist and slung it into the sink.

'What?' She was all innocent, eyebrows up, head on one side.

'Why are you blocking me? You've got to have some pain relief—even if you don't end up taking it, we have to have something in the house.'

'Oh Hel,' she drawled, baring her teeth in a grimace of fatigued superiority. 'It's par for the course, with the vitamin treatment. It's only the toxins—'

I cut across her. 'It's not the work. I'm glad to do that—I want to do it. But I'm scared when you're in this sort of pain and you haven't even got a pill that works. Maybe we should call the local palliative people. Just in case. So they know we exist.'

She raised both palms. 'No. I won't have anything to do with palliative.'

'Why,' I said dully, knowing the answer.

'Because it's the last thing before death.'

The word was in the room. I had dragged her to it. I looked at her there on the lavender sofa, fighting to hide her terror, and my heart contracted into a knot of pity, love and rage.

'Listen,' I said, in a voice I hardly recognised. 'You've come to my house. You've asked me to look after you for three weeks, and I will, because you're my friend and I love you—but I can't do it on my own. I'm so tired, and we're not even at the end of the first week. You've got to let me organise some help.'

White showed all round her pupils. 'I don't want anyone here but you.'

'All right then. Let's start with the drugs. If you don't want to see my GP, we'll get the Theodore people to recommend one in the city. And we'll do it today.'

I picked up the empty compost bucket and shoved it under the tap. Water roared into it. A small vase stood near me on the window ledge. I had never noticed before the intensity of its redness. It wasn't the sort of colour I was drawn to. Someone must have given it to me. When I turned round, Nicola was on her feet beside the couch. She lifted her head and looked me right in the face. I had forgotten how brown her eyes were. Her expression was calm and serious.

'Sorry, Helen,' she said. 'I'll be ready in ten minutes.'

~

That morning I didn't trust myself to face Colette. I waited in the street with the smokers while Nicola went up in the lift to ask about a GP. She came out with the name of one whose rooms were five minutes away, in Bourke Street. Nicola's neck was thrust forward again, her gait effortful: we walked slowly, and mounted the front steps of the building one-two, one-two, as toddlers do.

What sort of a nutcase would this new doctor be? But when she stepped into the waiting room and called Nicola's name, I saw her and rejoiced. She was an elegant, stick-thin woman pushing forty, in a narrow jacket and skirt that skimmed her wiry frame; her ankles and arches were so bony that she had to scuff her feet to keep her high-heeled sling-backs on. Her hair was as springy as a pot scrubber, and her face was darkly lit by a half-smile of ferocious irony. If Tuckey was Nicola's idea of a doctor, Naomi Caplan was mine.

I sat breathing in a forced rhythm while Nicola disappeared and the door closed. There was a silence of concentration, then the raising of the doctor's telephone voice in impatient authority. I waited. I read a *Women's Weekly* from cover to cover. A fax machine beeped and whirred. The doctor came charging out to the reception desk, snatched the page, and vanished again into the surgery. I could take any amount of this.

At last the two of them appeared. Nicola was holding a folded sheet of paper. Her smile was humble; the doctor's glinted with steel.

'Are you the friend?' said Dr Caplan to me. 'You won't get morphine at short notice from a city pharmacy. I'd advise you to go out to the Epworth Hospital. They'll fill it on the spot.' She nodded, and turned on her slender heel.

I wanted to run after her, babbling thanks and explanations: *It's not my fault. I'm not like her. I'm sensible!* The door clicked shut. Nicola toiled through her soft bag for a credit card. I went outside and stood in the air. The world sparkled unbearably bright.

We ordered a couple of vegetable juices in a cafe and sat quietly together at a table. When she looked at me it was with a face that was chastened, but closed. I didn't ask what had happened in the room. At ten she shuffled back to the Theodore. I took a tram along Wellington Parade to East Melbourne.

I was ready for a fight at the Epworth pharmacy. Stupid rage flared in me as the tram chugged up the rise past the Fitzroy Gardens. I remembered visiting my friend Damien in a famous teaching hospital when he was slogging into the last stages of a twenty-year cancer: he had broken a bone and was about to have it pinned. While I sat beside his bed, he began to sweat and shift under the sheet. It was half past five. He begged me to go to the nurses' station and remind them that in thirty minutes he would need his next dose of pills. Humouring him, I strolled up to the counter and passed on the superfluous message. I almost made a joke of it. But the nurse, a young man, was far from being offended. He breathed in through his teeth. 'Actually,' he said, 'we might be in trouble. The person with the key to the cupboard was supposed to be here two hours ago.'

A key? A cupboard? What century was this?

I asked him what the drug was. He named it. I remembered having seen three unopened packets of the stuff at Damien's house the night before, when I was looking for toothpaste in the bathroom. 'I don't suppose,' said the nurse, 'you could possibly go to his house and get them?'

Damien's place was half a mile from the hospital. There were no cabs. I ran. I tore along narrow lanes with my bag thumping on my back. His wife opened the door. We found the drugs. I grabbed the packets and turned around. I skidded into the ward at two minutes past six. 'Give them to me,' said Damien. 'Give them to me now.' I ran straight past him and threw them to the nurse. That was the last time I saw Damien. We never said goodbye. Three days later, he was dead.

I stepped off the tram and into the Epworth pharmacy.

A girl in a blue overall took the script, ran her

eyes over me, and said indifferently, 'It'll take about ten minutes.' I sat on a padded bench. Nicola's name was called. I signed the form. They handed me the cardboard packet. Back on Bridge Road I stood in the sun at the tram-stop, dizzy from the speed of the transaction.

What was all this anger? I needed to be kinder to her. Dying was frightening. But it was easier to imagine being tender when I had a packet of slow-release morphine capsules in my bag.

~

Nicola came home from the clinic that night shuddering again with cold and weakness. Eating was out of the question. She needed to wash but the thought of water hitting her skin was too much. I helped her into bed and sponged her face and neck, and then her feet, with a damp washer. Then she wanted to be left alone. She was the kind of person who loved to sleep in free streams of air: she used to boast that at her boarding school in the Southern Highlands the girls had slept winter and summer in a dormitory on an open veranda. Her house off Palm Beach welcomed every passing breeze; her life there had been a kind of glorified camping. But now she wanted the room dark and stuffy, the window shut tight.

I cooked myself a plate of curly pasta and ate it in front of the TV. Halfway through the news I was asleep on the couch. The phone rang and I blundered to answer it. A young woman with a soft, anxious voice asked for Nicola.

'She's not feeling the best tonight,' I said. 'Could you ring in the morning?'

'Oh, please let me speak to her,' said the caller. 'I only heard today that she's ill. I'm Hamish's daughter—I know she'll want to hear from me. Couldn't I just have a quick word?'

I carried the cordless along the hall to Nicola's door. The lamp was on; I thought I heard her groan.

I opened the door and held out the phone. 'Hamish's daughter?'

She shook her head and raised one palm. I did some fast talking and hung up.

'It's my shoulder again,' said Nicola. 'My neck. And there's a new pain. In the middle of my belly. I'm scared it might be my liver.'

I brought in one of the morphine capsules and

raised it like a wafer between thumb and forefinger. She looked at it suspiciously.

'Nicola. Take it.'

'I don't want to get addicted.'

'You won't get addicted. It'll help you go to sleep.' I poured a glass of water.

She shook her head. 'I had the vitamin C again today. That must be why my shoulder's hurting more. It's the toxins tearing their way out.'

I put the pill and the glass on the bedside table. 'OK. Can I get you something else?'

'I feel a bit nauseated. I don't suppose there's any lemonade?'

I wheeled my bike down the side path and sped in the dark to the milk bar. Yes, the light was on. The young proprietor was mopping the floor. How did he maintain his lovely courtesy, in a job with such punishing hours? Next to the register stood a flat box of chocolate bullets. He and his pregnant wife must have spent hours out the back there with the lollies loose between them on the table, raking them in tens onto squares of cling wrap and sealing each tiny packet into a peak with sticky-tape. I grabbed one, then pulled a bottle of lemonade out of the wall fridge. Pedalling home along the empty street I steered the bike with one hand and shovelled bullets into my mouth with the other. The lemonade rolled about in the basket.

She accepted a glass of it, but the bubbles were still too strenuous, and she sat up in bed with her head forward like a tortoise, waiting for the fizz to die down.

'I was thinking today,' she said. 'I should write something about the Theodore Institute. It might help them. They need publicity.'

I couldn't meet her eye.

'I don't understand,' I said, 'how they can go on giving you the vitamin C treatment, when they know it has this terrible effect on you. What's it supposed to do?'

'But Helen,' she whispered. 'It's the same with chemo and radiation. Nobody knows how they work, either, but people still do them.'

I had no answer. I sat in the corner on the hard chair.

'Darling,' she murmured after a while. 'I think I will take the morphine now.'

~

Forty minutes later I heard her stirring. She was sitting up again, with her shoulders bowed right down over her knees.

'What is it, old stick?'

'I'm sure it's just the bad stuff coming out. In a minute I might try lying on my stomach.'

'All right. What'll I do?'

She was silent. I waited beside the bed. Half a minute passed.

'I think I'll try it now.'

I stepped forward. How do you roll someone over when what's hurting is her shoulder, her neck, her belly? Where do you take hold? I stood there helpless in my ignorance. In a while I heard her draw a determined breath. Expelling it in a series of hard grunts, she got herself on to her side, asked me to slide a pillow under her, and collapsed on to it belly down.

~

Soon after midnight she called me. Her bed was soaked with sweat. The pain seemed to have abated, though, so I sent her to lie on the couch in the big back room while I changed the sheets. When I came out she was propped against the cushions, dopey from the morphine, but lucid.

'I was lying in there,' she said, 'thinking fuck. I shouldn't have asked that GP for the weakest pill.'

She asked for the weakest pill.

My legs sagged. I sat down on the arm of the couch with my load of wet bedding.

'Nicola,' I said. 'I've got something to say. I don't think I can go on with this, unless you let me call the palliative people on Monday.'

She went rigid. 'I told you—I don't need that.'

'It's not the angel of death,' I said. 'It's just some girls in a car.'

'I said no.'

'If we got ourselves on their list, they'd come to the house if we needed them. They can help people get through the night. They're like the district nurse.'

She reared up on the cushions. 'I don't need a nurse.'

I let the bedding drop to the floor. Then I kicked it all the way to the laundry and stuffed it into the machine. Out there I folded the ironing board and stood it against the wall. I sorted a basket of dry clothes. I stayed among the equipment for imposing cleanliness and order until I had got a grip on myself. When I emerged, she spoke loftily from the couch, without opening her eyes.

'I've decided what to do. I'm going to take a serviced apartment. Or move into some mad little hotel in South Yarra. I'll only be down here for another fortnight. I don't want to be a burden to anyone.'

I leaned against the fridge. The lumpy magnets, with their lists and reminders, pressed into my back. I turned and rearranged them into a rustic pattern: the lemons, the painted roses, the two golden bees that Hughie loved. I carried the hot water bottle to the kettle, filled it, and handed it to her on the couch. Her eyes were still closed. In the spare room I made up her bed again and puffed the pillows. Then I trudged back to my own room and crept under the quilt.

How had I got myself into this?

Death was in my house. Its rules pushed new life away with terrible force. I longed for the children next door, their small, determined bodies through which vitality surged. It was barely one o'clock and I was wide awake and staring-eyed. I thought I could hear movement in the kitchen, perhaps a voice murmuring, but it was a matter of urgency that I should get to sleep before two, the hour at which the drought, the refugee camps, the dying planet, and all the faults and meannesses of my character would arrive to haunt me.

On the bedside table lay the manuscript of a novel by a Vietnamese woman that I was supposed to have read last week. I picked a page at random. The characters seemed to be working in a sweatshop, thanklessly sewing trash under the savage eye of a supervisor. 'In empty times like this,' the narrator remarked, 'singing a half-remembered song helps to make the time pass.'

My ukulele was gathering dust on the floor. I drew it out of its case by the neck and cradled it for a while. Its stiff woody curves comforted me. It was still in tune. The bedroom door was open, but the morphine would surely have kicked in by now. I sat up in bed and played softly. Under my breath I sang 'Tennessee Waltz' and 'After the Ball': slow tunes in three-four time that gave me a chance to get my fingers on to the next chord and still keep the beat. Then I closed my mouth and just brushed the strings, barely making a sound.

I was laying the uke back in its case when she called out down the hall.

'Hel?'

'I'm here.'

'Goodnight. We'll call the palliative on Monday.'

6

GOD BLESS morphine. In the morning she was in bright spirits, affectionate in a slightly guilty way. At breakfast she swallowed another pill and sat at the table gazing out at the garden.

'It's a nice day,' she cried, with a hectic eagerness. 'We should get stuck into the garden. Do some weeding.'

'Oh, bugger that,' I said. 'Let's go to the nursery. You can tell me what natives to buy.'

The day flowed by in modest pastimes. We read, we dozed, we drove to the video shop and the supermarket. At the nursery on the banks of the Maribyrnong she made me buy grevilleas 'for their future dusty pinkness'. She found an envelope of nasturtium seeds in my pantry, took them outside and pushed them into the dirt with her thumbs, all along the front path.

Bessie tapped on the kitchen window and asked for yoghurt with nuts.

'I'm in a flamenco show tomorrow afternoon,' she shouted. 'On a stage.'

I handed the food through the crack of the back door and she ate it on the veranda, smiling at us over her shoulder through the glass, then ran off to the gap in the fence, leaving the empty bowl and spoon on the doormat.

Before dinner Nicola made a couple of magisterial gin and tonics and we drank them in front of the TV, to armour ourselves against the news of the world. Later we watched the DVD she had chosen, *Million Dollar Baby*. We loved the girl boxer leaping out of her corner with her fists up: *let me at you!* I privately thought the ending was sentimental; Nicola cried; and then we both praised Hilary Swank to the skies. This was the way we had always been together. It was easy.

She took the morphine according to the instructions on the packet. In the absence of the intravenous vitamin C it worked its magic, making the night brief.

But on Sunday my friend Peggy, with whom Nicola was remotely acquainted, called to invite us for morning tea.

'That's nice of her,' said Nicola. 'I thought you two had fallen out again.'

'Oh, that's our style. We get over it. We're going to Europe in December, for a couple of weeks.'

'Europe?' She paused. 'How divine.'

We drove to Fitzroy. When Peggy, chic and smooth-haired, opened her front door, Nicola leapt through it and straight into the kitchen, grinning wildly, spraying compliments and exclamations in her poshest accent: it was a tremendous performance of being alive. It scraped on my nerves. A bowl of walnuts stood on the sideboard. I grabbed a couple and cracked them in my palms. I ate the first few kernels, but the cracking was so gratifying that after I had eaten enough I kept going, trying to find each nut's weak point, grinding the hard shells against each other till they split.

When Nicola paused for breath, Peggy ushered us out into the garden. We sat under a roof of blossoming white roses whose petals sprinkled down on to the embroidered tablecloth. She served us pleasantly and with grace: biscuits and a cake, coffee, and interesting kinds of tea. She and Nicola spoke with sighs and wry smiles about the difficulties of caring for their mothers, queenly dames in their nineties who were often balefully demanding. Mine, who had been small and sad and beaten, was already five years dead. I sat and listened.

'So,' said Peggy at last. 'How's it all going, over there?'

'Well,' Nicola began, leaning forward with a smile so glassy it tinkled. 'It's all going brilliantly. Helen's a wonderfully severe matron. But we've had to get hold of some morphine the last few days. You see, at the Theodore Institute, which is marvellous, they give me a certain intravenous vitamin C treatment every second day.'

She was settling in. Irritated, I tipped my head back and took a proper look at the roses. Quite a few of them were already drying up and drooping. The secateurs lay near me on the windowsill. I grabbed them and made a few furtive passes at the blossoms within reach.

'It does knock one around somewhat,' Nicola went on, 'and I sometimes come home a wee bit under the weather.'

I felt my lips pursing. I stood up and moved away from the table, flexing the clipper as I went. An old wooden ladder was leaning against the shed wall. The little building was wreathed in the climbing roses, and every third flower was ready to be snipped.

'Of course I know I'll always come through it unscathed. I know it's only the vitamin C savaging the tumours and driving them out. But,' she said with a gay laugh, 'to my utter astonishment, and to my shame for being so pathetically selfish, I was absolutely and totally unaware that to poor Hel it was a horrendous spectacle.'

Clenching my teeth, I mounted the first three rungs and attacked the upper layers of the plant. *Poor Hel.* The blossoms fell from my blades in a steady shower of white. The brick paving was strewn with them.

'So, late last night I rang my divine niece Iris, who I'd been staying with in Sydney for the last six months, and asked her if she'd found the shivering scary—and she said, "What are you talking about, woman? It's terrifying. I was shitting myself every time. You look as if you're about to die."' Her voice rose and broke in a trill of social laughter.

I forced the safety catch shut on the secateurs and climbed down to the ground. Nicola moved along the bench to make room for me. Peggy filled my cup and pushed it across to me, without meeting my eye.

'And so,' said Nicola, swigging the dregs of her tea, 'we're going to ring the palliative care people tomorrow. I know we'll never need to call them out. I'm sure the treatment's shifting the cancer—within ten days I'll be fighting fit and on the mend. The palliative thing's just so Hel won't feel completely alone and without back-up—my poor old Hel.'

Blood rushed into my face. Nicola's eyebrows shot up to her hairline. She bared her teeth at me and laughed again, a melodious, mocking gust of it from deep in her throat.

'It's the nights,' I said, in a strangled voice. 'The nights are long.'

Peggy glanced at me. Horrified sympathy passed along her eye-beams. It weakened me. A huge wave of fatigue rinsed me from head to foot. I was afraid I would slide off the bench and measure my length among the cut roses. At the same time a chain of metallic thoughts went clanking through my mind, like the first dropping of an anchor. Death will not be denied. To try is grandiose. It drives madness into the soul. It leaches out virtue. It injects poison into friendship, and makes a mockery of love.

~

After lunch at home Nicola lay down to rest, and I drove across town to the Hogar Español. Not wanting to be an embarrassment to my daughter and her husband, or to go home with crowd germs, I stayed at the back near the door. The Spanish families at the tables went on shouting and drinking with a cheerful noise, even once the old men with guitars across their knees had started to strum and the old women, their dyed hair piled high with combs and flowers, had set up their fierce clapping. On the ill-lit stage Bessie and her companions paraded forward in a bloc, their spines erect, their shoulders back and chests open. They flung up their arms, they twirled their wrists and fingers high and low. To the harsh cries of the singers, they battered the floor with their hard-heeled shoes and lashed about them with the deep, crimson flounces of their skirts. Tears burst from my eyes and I covered my face.

~

Before Nicola could leave for the clinic on Monday morning, I called the Mercy palliative service. The voice of the woman who answered the phone was calm and friendly. Like Peggy's glance of sympathy under the climbing roses, it almost undid me. I stammered out a truncated version of our situation.

'Can I ask,' she said, 'what's the actual diagnosis?'

I carried the cordless to the stove, where Nicola was lowering an egg into a pan of boiling water.

'I've got the palliative lady here,' I said. 'She needs to know what your actual diagnosis is.'

She paused with her back to me, then turned, took the phone, and launched with courteous efficiency on the same history I had heard her offer to Dr Tuckey that first night at the clinic. I crossed the veranda and wandered down the yard, inspecting the broad beans and herbs. The air around plants was supposed to have beneficial properties, wasn't it? I pushed in and stood breathing among the leafy stalks. Sheets and clothes from the day before were still hanging on the line. I unpegged them and slung them over my shoulder. The voice in the kitchen stopped. I stepped back across the threshold into a blast of Nicola's white glare.

'They wanted to come out this weekend,' she snarled. 'To assess me.' She slammed the phone against the stove-top. 'Oh, look at this. My fucking egg's broken. I hate a broken egg.'

Something violent sizzled in me. I forced myself to walk through the room with my eyes down.

~

At lunchtime she phoned me from the clinic. She was merry, and warm. Guess what! Professor Theodore was back from China. She liked him! And he'd had a wonderful idea—that after the vitamin C treatment she should stay lying down in one of the rooms all afternoon, to see if the cold shudders happened. So he could 'monitor' them. Not only that—he'd suggested she should try coffee enemas. He thought they might lessen her dependence on the morphine. So she was going to pop out, before they plugged in the vitamin C, to buy some organic coffee. Did I know where she could get some in the city?

Wasn't there a sort of light machine gun called an Uzi?

'Try David Jones' Food Hall,' I said.

'Thanks, darling. Don't bother to cook anything tonight. I won't be home till after eight. There's a two-hour lecture here that I'm supposed to go to—byeeeee.'

I sat on the back step and wrestled with the blackest, most glowering scepticism. I didn't want to be a bigot. How could I detach from this? Serve her, yet detach? I rang my sister Lucy, the religious one, the former nurse, and arranged to meet her at the Waiters' Club at six o'clock.

~

That afternoon a woman from the Mercy palliative called me. No, they were not just for cancer patients or the dying. They were part of the free District Nursing Service. She had offered to come over on

Saturday morning to meet us both, but apparently Nicola was not so keen. Her name was Carmel, and yes, she had a moment to talk with me now.

I rattled off the short version. When I trailed away she left a tactful pause before she spoke. Western medicine, she said, when it had reached the end of what it had to offer, would usually throw in the towel and say so; but outfits like the Theodore Institute tended to keep people linked to them in cloudy hope, right to the end.

Right to the end.

'Does Nicola have any religious beliefs?'

I went quiet.

When my former husband had first introduced me to her, fifteen years ago, I took to Nicola at once. Everything about her, the way she placed food on the table or rolled a cigarette or slung a length of coloured fabric around her neck, was carefree and graceful. In her presence, things slowed down and opened out. I admired the Indian-tinged style of her house and the things she wore. I did spot a couple of photos of a hot-eyed guru lurking in a dark corner of the book-shelves, but she never referred to him, and I didn't ask. I assumed she was an old hand at meditation and yoga, and that if she had any particular beliefs they were so ingrained that she didn't need to speak about them, just as I kept quiet about my adventures in churches.

Then in recent years, shortly before she became ill, Buddhist terms had entered her discourse. She knew how to pronounce *rinpoche* and where to get a ticket when the famous ones were coming to town. She subjected herself to ten-day vipassana boot camps in the Blue Mountains: her accounts of these speechless ordeals were shaped to make me laugh, but she always came back to the city elated. She referred casually to weekend teachings, and to new friends with names that sounded made up; she had taken to wearing little thread bangles, or a string of knobbly, dark red wooden beads. So I imagined that somewhere in her free-wheeling nature she was quietly equipping herself, as everyone must, with whatever it is one needs to die.

'It depends,' I said at last, 'on what you would call religious.'

'It's just that in my work,' said Carmel, 'I've learnt that there are people who never, ever face the fact that death's coming to them. They go on fighting right up to their last breath.' She paused. 'And it is one way of doing it.'

Again the vast weakness sifted through me. I saw that I had been working towards a glorious moment of enlightenment, when Nicola would lay down her manic defences; when she would look around her, take a deep breath, and say, 'All right. I'm going to die. I bow to it. Now I will live the rest of my life in truth.'

'And from what you're telling me,' said the nurse, in her soft, unreproachful voice, 'I'm wondering whether you should try to accept that Nicola might be one of these. That she might. . .die in this state.'

~

I came up the steps from Parliament Station and spotted Lucy cruising into Little Collins Street on her touring bike. It had big, reliable-looking panniers and, although the sun had not set, she had turned on one of those fast-blinking tail-lights that illuminate the countryside for miles around. By the time I caught up with her, she was chaining the bike to a railing. Even as early as six we weren't the first customers at the Waiters' Club: at the top of the wooden stairs, the joint was jumping. We ordered a couple of grilled flounder. The waitress brought wine in tumblers and I began to gulp it down. Lucy saw from the look on my face that I was going to have to hog the conversation. I started with the enemas.

'If she's constipated,' she said, 'an enema could move stuff along—that might relieve the pain in her belly.'

'Yes, I can see that. I'm the last person to have a problem with enemas. But coffee ones? Is coffee good for pain? And apparently the coffee has to be organic.'

'For God's sake! It's going up her bum—isn't instant good enough?'

'The boss of the clinic said it might reduce her reliance on morphine.'

'What reliance? Is she shovelling it down? Bombed out of her brain? Queuing up first thing every morning at the doctor's?'

Oh, the crazed relief of dobbing, of disloyalty.

We drank; we devoured the flat, pale fish; we polished off a salad and a pile of pancakes with lemon juice, and while we ate I jabbered and Lucy split her sides. When the espresso arrived we both calmed down, and she began to analyse.

'I'm not surprised she laughed at your fear. Laughter like that's a sort of aggression, don't you think? You're the messenger with the bad news. She'd like to kill you for trying to carry it to her. She's fighting to keep it away—as if the message itself might kill her on the spot.'

'So why did she choose me to stay with?'

'She must trust you. You could take it as a compliment.'

'I do. But there are clinics in Sydney where you can get these loony treatments. She's got heaps of friends up there—people from long before I met her. They'd have no trouble at all with ozone and cupping. And they wouldn't keep pulling the rug out from under her. I'm scared she's going to turn me into a horrible, punitive mother.'

Lucy drained the tiny cup of coffee. 'When I worked with cancer patients, years ago, there was a man I used to sit with sometimes, who was dying, but his family was pretending he was going to get better. He got attached to me, I think. I liked him a lot. We used to have long, existential conversations and I looked forward to them. On this particular day it was past the end of my shift—I was tired, my feet were sore, I should have been out of there already. I just popped my head round his door on my way home, and he hit me with it: "I haven't got long to go, have I." I wasn't prepared—I gave a pat answer. He turned away and said in a bored, dismissive tone, "If you say so." I was upset. He'd given me an opening and I'd missed it. I went off feeling I'd failed him. But when I got home I realised it didn't matter how pathetic my response was. Because there was a silent understanding between us. There was nobody else in that room with him, no one else in his life at that time, who would "say so"!

She smiled at me with her head on one side. I only just bit back the words, 'Gee, you look like Mum': this was not considered a compliment between us.

'You mean I have to say so and yet not say so?'

'Maybe she's picked you for that exact job.' She screwed up her paper napkin and shoved it into a glass. 'Or maybe…consciously or otherwise…she's come to your house to die.'

I looked up in dismay. 'But I'm going away in

December. I've paid for my ticket.'

'Don't panic,' said Lucy, undoing the clasp of her fat leather purse. 'No one can plan these things. Stage four can go on for years.'

'But you don't really think that's why she came, do you?'

'It's a long way to come for a treatment. And she sounds as if she's getting quite a grip on you. That's when mothers get punitive. When their shift never ends.'

She laughed, and pointed at my hands clasped on the tabletop. The knuckles were white.

'You're fighting,' she said, 'to hold on to what's been precious in this friendship. But you don't want to go crazy, or lose your grip on reality the way she has. It is a sort of madness. And it's quite common.'

We split the bill, piling notes and coins on the sticky tabletop, and thumped down the stairs into the lane.

'Do you ever go to communion?' she asked as she unchained her bike from the car-park railing.

'No. I can't find a church I can stand. I hate it when they're ponderous.'

'Go to the Catholics, then. They really rip along.'

We laughed. A warm breeze puffed among the rubbish bins.

'Hey Luce. Can I ask you something? Would you bless me?'

She paused, with the straps of her helmet dangling beside her smooth cheeks. She made as if to take it off.

'Leave it on,' I said. 'It makes you look official.'

'Sometimes,' she said, 'there's only one prayer to say. *Lamb of God. You take away the sin of the world.*'

I stood in front of her, listening and nodding. She put her palm against my forehead. *Have mercy on us.* Then she made a little twirl with her thumb, maybe the sign of the cross, I couldn't see.

'May the Lord bless you and keep you,' she said.

'Thank you.'

'And make His face to shine upon you.'

She buckled up her helmet, flicked on her lights, kissed me on both cheeks, and pedalled away in a westerly direction.

7

WHEN I walked into the kitchen, the lamp was on and Nicola was standing at the bench, chewing, with one hand plunged into a large, squat, brown paper bag.

'Look at these!'

She held out a cupped palm full of creamy white pips. 'They're apricot kernels. You know—the bits you smash the stones to get out, and put it in the jam to make it set?'

'Pectin?'

'Laetrile. It attacks cancer, Professor Theodore says. I have to eat twenty a day.' She raised her palm to her mouth and nibbled from it with her front teeth. 'Have some.'

I picked one out of the bag: there must have been two kilos of the things. It had a peculiar flavour; delicious, but wild and with a distant after-taste, like something that might be poisonous if you got the quantities wrong. I ate several more. She gave me a companionable smile and we stood there, munching.

'How did you go today?'

'They plugged me into the vitamin C,' she said, 'and I lay there all afternoon waiting for the cold shudders and sweats to start. Not a squeak. Not a quiver. I felt a complete idiot. Like when you take your car to the mechanic and suddenly it's running perfectly.'

We started to laugh.

'Did you ask them about the pain?'

Once more she brushed it aside. 'Lay off, Hel—these people deal with cancer every day. Pain's not something they want to hear about.'

I let it pass. I had to learn to let it pass.

'Remember Marj from Broken Hill?' she said cheerfully. 'The bald lady in the little black toque, that you liked? Do you know how she heard about the Theodore? In a seance. And that's why she came all this way. And next week some people are arriving from Canada! To do the treatments!'

She grinned at me, stuffing in another handful of pips. Mine were starting to make me feel a bit sick. I dropped them back in the bag. Under the bench I found a huge jar with a red screw lid, and tipped the kernels into it. Packed behind the clear glass they radiated a meaningless glamour, like a photo in a lifestyle magazine.

'The clinic's closed tomorrow,' she said. 'It's the Melbourne Cup. How about we go to the movies?'

~

The morning was grey and gentle, with doves. The racecourse was half a mile from my house, and in Cup Week the roads of our suburb were packed morning and evening, so we chose a movie that was screening across the river in South Yarra, and took our lunch to the Botanic Gardens. The sun came out, the day grew bright. We chose a palm tree that cast a shadow of perfect roundness, and settled on the grass within its perimeter. I laid out our sandwiches and our bottles of water. Nicola always looked relaxed when she sat on the ground: her hips were looser in their sockets than other people's. Her long legs sprawled gracefully under her faded sky-blue cotton skirt.

'This whole thing's hard on you, Helen, isn't it,' she said.

'Harder than I'd expected.'

'What's the worst part? Is it the sweating?'

Here was my chance. 'No—it's feeling we're in bad faith with each other.'

Her head swung round. 'Bad faith? Us?'

'You won't like to hear this.'

'Go on.'

She took a neat bite of a sandwich, and shifted so we were sitting side by side, facing in the same direction. By breaking eye contact she freed me, as one is free to spew up true things in a car on a long night drive.

'I've got serious doubts,' I said, 'about the clinic.'

She let her gaze rove over the soft, well-kept lawn that sloped all the way down to the lake.

'I can't say I'm surprised,' she said, with a small laugh. 'I always knew it wouldn't be your speed. Darling, don't worry. I know you do your best.'

'Yes, but I'm getting the same vibe off these treatments as I did off that cabbage juice guy up in the Hunter Valley. I can't help feeling they're charlatans. Either that, or they're deluded.'

Calmly she shook her head, smiling, chewing, always smiling. 'You saved me from the biochemist— I'm eternally grateful for that. But he was a crook. These people are different. I believe in them. Their theories are solidly based. And they really, really care about me.'

'So where was the boss,' I said with difficulty, 'that morning you arrived? He told you to come a week early, and then he stood you up.'

'It's his research, Hel. He has to keep abreast of international developments.'

I bored on, miserably. 'What about the rest of them, then? They're hardly what you'd call impressive, are they? How can you trust those people?'

'But Helen,' she said, turning her face to me in earnest surprise. 'I have to trust them. I don't have a choice. I've got to keep myself revved up and directed and purposeful.'

'That's what's hardest for me. The revving.'

She looked down at the grass. I was hurting her.

'But it's the only way,' she said. 'If I don't have faith, the only alternative is to lie down and say OK, I give up. I'm dying. Cancer, come and get me.'

A dry breeze puffed up the slope. It lifted her hair and showed the pitiful thinness of her neck. I put down my sandwich and grabbed her hands.

'Nicola,' I said. 'Those are the two absolute extremes.'

'Yes, well, that's what I'm facing.'

Her tone was almost huffy. She wouldn't meet my eye. She tried to take back her hands, but I hung on. I squeezed them, I shook them.

'There's got to be a path between the two,' I said. 'Can't we try to find it?'

She pulled away from me and stared out at the lake.

'I can't give up,' she said. 'I won't give up.'

'Would it have to be giving up, though? Could you think about taking it one day at a time? Like they do at AA? Not say *I'm dying* or *I'm not dying*—just say *I'm alive today?*'

'You don't understand. It's different for you.'

'Why is it different?' I said. 'Aren't we all the same, before...' *Before death* or *before God* was what I wanted to say, but it would have sounded melodramatic.

'You've done things,' she said. 'You've worked. You've been married.'

'Married?' I almost laughed. 'Those train wrecks?'

'You've made a family. I've wasted my life,' she said. 'Look at me. I'm sixty-five. What have I got to show for it?'

Her mouth writhed, but she controlled it.

'I've had amazing good fortune,' she said. 'Born with reasonable good looks. A family with money. A few talents. But I threw it all away. I made nothing of myself. I was sloppy. I never stuck at anything. I failed and just kept moving. I wasted my good luck. I pissed it up against the wall. It's no wonder I've run out of it now.'

I could have poured out a thousand flattering protests, but her back was bolt upright, her hands were folded, and in profile she looked so dignified that it would have been impertinent to try to comfort her. So I sat beside her on the grass, and followed her gaze; and the lake, the lawn, the elms, the sailing flat-bottomed clouds, and the summer day itself darkened and disintegrated before our eyes.

~

The cinema was quiet and empty, and so were we, by the time we took our places. The film was Sally Potter's *Yes*, with dialogue in iambic pentameter. We saw at once that in this country it could only be a commercial disaster. Our bruised hearts rushed to it in solidarity, and it came to our rescue. We sighed, we cried. We poked each other with our elbows. We snorted with laughter behind our hands. We wanted to be Joan Allen, or at least to stride about in her silky garments and classy little Italian knits. And we cheered when the cleaning woman delivered straight to camera the film's closing lines:

> . . . *in fact I think, I guess,*
> *That No does not exist. There's only Yes.*

'Ah Helen,' said Nicola as we sped back along Punt Road. 'That film was dropped into our laps by some god or other. I'd like to write the director a fan letter. And this very night I'm going to give myself a coffee enema.'

~

Just as we were about to open a bottle of wine and slouch in front of the TV for the racing news, my son-in-law Mitch and his friend Locky from Torquay emerged from my back shed, where they had been working together on their crazy paintings, and came to the kitchen door: two smiling surfers with clear, bright eyes and hair like straw.

'Can we come in?' said Mitch shyly. 'My cold's better.'

Nicola liked young men, and they liked her. She favoured these two with a kind and questioning smile, as they popped their stubbies and settled into armchairs.

'I know you'll tell us if this is out of line,' Mitch went on. 'But I happened to mention to Locky that you were sick, Nicola, and he wondered if...'

'I'm a sort of consultant,' said Locky, 'for a company that sells, uhm...'

He laid a bag on the floor and pulled out of it several flat strips of a rubbery, silver-grey material. He spread them on the coffee table. Some were circular, some were foot-shaped. We looked at them politely.

'What it's for,' said Locky, 'is it puts your immune

system back into its optimal state. So everything in your body's running smoothly.'

Nicola shifted in her seat. The wattage of her smile decreased. Mitch flicked her a nervous glance. The door opened and Bessie bounded in. Her cold, she said, was gone; but her fair hair was tightly plaited and pinned in a coronet, in the style that betokened an attack of nits. She sat on her father's knee and bent her brow over the objects. A short silence fell.

'I know it sounds weird,' said Locky. He looked up at Nicola and flashed his dazzling teeth. 'I never dreamt I'd be sitting in somebody's lounge room with a bag full of magnets.'

I laughed.

'Magnets!' said Nicola, sparking up.

'They replicate the earth's magnetic field,' said Locky. 'I don't exactly understand how they work, but I swear they do. You ladies got any ice in your fridge?'

I brought him a cube of it and he set it down on one of the circular shapes. The ice began at once to melt: water pooled around it at unnatural speed on the grey rubbery surface, then overflowed on to the tabletop. Locky whipped a tissue out of his pocket and mopped it up.

Bessie's mouth was hanging open. 'That should go in a magic show!'

'It's like watching a cartoon,' said Nicola.

Mitch looked happily from face to face. 'Remember how my feet used to ache, Helen?' he said. 'I put the insoles in my shoes and now they never hurt at all.'

'They make mattress covers too,' said Locky. 'We sleep on one at home. I used to have terrible back pain. But now it's gone. And if I ever leave one of the mats on the floor, I come back and find the bloody dogs are lying on it.'

We were all laughing, sitting forward.

'Can it do arthritis?' I asked. 'My big toe joints hurt like hell.'

Locky handed me a pair of insoles, far too big for me. I laid them on the carpet, pulled off my sensible red sandals, and placed my bare feet on the rubbery stuff. Its surface was oddly pleasing: smooth and soft, but with an underlying firmness. I sat waiting for whatever it was to take effect. My eyes came to rest on the leg of the kitchen table. Locky talked on, in his drawling, slangy way, about the excellence of the company's special silver-stone filter: the water it produced, he said, had a sort of silky quality. His kids drank it all day, couldn't be stopped, whereas before, they'd had to be forced to swallow even a single glass of tap water. His voice faded to a pleasant, soothing element of the ambient noise. I was quite alert, not at all sleepy; yet when he dashed out the front and lugged in a sample filter from the boot of his car, I had to guide my mind back to the matter in hand.

Nicola, meanwhile, sat hunched in the white armchair, listening to Locky's tales of exemplary hydration and freedom from pain, with her eyebrows up and her smiling mouth half open. I almost laughed: she looked so lovably innocent and gormless, like a beldame at a travelling minstrel show.

By the time Locky stood up to leave, we had agreed to take a big water filter and various items of bedding for a fortnight's obligation-free trial. Nicola, a convert, declared she was going to buy me the filter for five hundred dollars. I had paid up front for a pair of the magic insoles, and was already trying to trim them down to fit my sandals. As the back door clicked behind Bessie and the men, I looked up and saw with surprise that outside it was already dark. They had been entertaining us for two hours.

~

As it happened, I knew how to administer a neat, simple and clean enema: I had once undergone a course of colonic irrigations at a health spa on the island of Koh Samui. My account of that week had sent us into endless laughing fits; but Nicola seemed to have forgotten it now, and this did not seem the moment to start throwing my weight around. Still, when I saw her brewing the organic coffee in the kitchen after dinner, I said tentatively, 'Do you need a hand to set it up? I can...'

She shook her head, too busy to listen.

'I wonder, though,' I said, as she forged off to the bathroom with the equipment. 'Is it a good idea to have a coffee enema at bedtime? You don't think the caffeine might keep you awake?'

'Why on earth would it do that, darling?' she said breezily. 'I won't be drinking it—I'll only be putting it up my bum.'

I backed off. From behind the closed door I heard thumping and splashing, then a silence, then a volley of curses. I went to my room and got into bed.

My mobile rang. It was my friend Rosalba in Newcastle. For ten minutes we boasted about our grandchildren, taking it in turns and offering each other full attention. I told her I had a friend staying with me who was very sick with cancer, and that this meant I hadn't spent as much time with the kids as usual.

'Ah, poor woman,' said Rosalba. 'But you say she lives in Sydney? Why she staying with you?'

I explained about the clinic and its treatments. She clicked her tongue. 'Three weeks. That's a long time. Where's her family?'

It was a simple question, but I hesitated.

'She not married?'

'No.'

'No children?'

'No. I've never got to know her family. She's got a couple of nieces she's close to. Some great-nephews that she loves. An ancient mother. And an older sister who lives in the country, with troubles of her own.'

A light stream of silent incomprehension, even disapproval, flowed down the line. I began to flail around.

'She's what you'd call a bohemian, I guess.'

'Bohemian? What's that?'

'Someone who believes in freedom. Thinks it's important to be an artist. That sort of thing. Not interested in getting married, or having families in the usual way.'

'Freedom?' said Rosalba. 'Huh. When you sick, you go to your family.'

By midnight, when I went to the toilet, a bucketful of soaking towels was standing in the bath, and the whole house smelled like an espresso bar.

At dawn Nicola stumbled into the kitchen, haggard and shaky. She had hardly slept. I served the breakfast without comment. Soon she had the smile pasted on and her eyes staring wide. In future, she said, she would do the enemas only in the mornings.

Next morning she emerged from the bathroom dishevelled and exasperated.

'I don't think I'll do any more. It's so hard to hold your sphincter shut and get up off the floor and on to the toilet in time to let go—I'm fed up with washing towels. I wish there was a way to get my bum right over the toilet, so I could do it in a more relaxed way.'

In a very small voice I said, 'There is. I tried to

tell you on Tuesday, but you wouldn't listen.'

She stopped and looked at me, half smiling, abashed. It was a hollow victory.

~

That evening she came home from the clinic in high spirits, and reported that she had been seen by a new bloke: 'he was a real doctor.'

'How could you tell?'

'Oh,' she said, 'just by looking. He said that the increased pain is definitely being caused by the treatments jazzing the cancer up.'

I listened, and nodded, and smiled because she was pleased. But I wondered what he had really said to her, and in what language, for *jazzing up* sounded like one of her own expressions, drawn from the same posh, old-fashioned lexicon as *carry on, crash hot, my divine niece* and *some mad little hotel in South Yarra.*

~

The low dose of morphine was losing its grip. That night Nicola was in steady pain, concentrated in her neck and shoulder. She came up with an inexhaustible flow of bright explanations: she had twanged a muscle turning over in bed; her usual thick flannelette nightie was in the wash; a breeze had come in through the window and chilled her shoulder. When she talked like that I thought my head was going to burst. But we slogged on. Somehow we slept a little; somehow the daylight came.

8

ON FRIDAY morning Nicola set off for the clinic pale with fatigue but happy and excited: the *divine niece* Iris and her boyfriend Gab were to fly down from Sydney that evening, and would stay with us till Sunday night. I pedalled to the shops and prepared a vegetarian meal, then hauled out the double futon and set it up on its slatted base in the room with the bookshelves: reading lamp, flower in a bottle, folded towels.

Towards five o'clock a taxi pulled up at my gate. A tall, thin, very long-legged young woman in loose cotton clothes stepped out, followed by an equally thin and tall young man: they might almost have been siblings, except that her hair was a mass of wild brown curls and his was smooth and black. They hesitated with their bags under the plane trees, looking for the house number. At the sight of their shy, intelligent faces, my weariness and fright overwhelmed me. I rushed down the front path and threw myself into the divine niece's arms.

I got the Absolut out of the freezer and the three of us hunkered down over the shot glasses, trying to make a plan before Nicola got home.

'I suggested to her the other night,' said Iris, 'when she called me about the shuddering fits, that she should think about coming back to Sydney after two weeks instead of three. Did she tell you?'

'Not a word,' I said.

'I was appalled by the idea of her staying three weeks with you. She hasn't the faintest clue what she asks of people. That enraging brightness—even twenty-four hours can drive you round the twist. But she jacks up if you put things to her directly. So I thought, if I booked her a ticket on the sly and just discreetly planted the idea on the phone, it might sprout during the week, and by Sunday she'd be ready to come home with me and Gab. But she wouldn't have a bar of it. She kept saying, "I know I'm going

119

to get better—and if I don't keep doing the treat-ments, I'll die.'"

We grimaced at each other.

'What are the treatments, exactly?' asked Gab.

I tried to describe them without prejudice, taking into account what I imagined their beliefs about alternative medicine might be. But when I got to the ozone sauna with the electrodes, they could no longer keep straight faces. We squirmed on the couches, unable to look at each other. In the middle of our spasms, the back door opened and Bessie stepped in.

'Hello young girl,' said Iris, wiping her eyes on her sleeve. 'Who are you? Come here.'

Bessie marched straight to the couch and squeezed herself in between the visitors. She subjected them to a thorough sartorial examination, turning her head smoothly and scanning them up and down. Iris put an arm round Bessie's shoulders and we went on talking and laughing.

The phone rang. Bessie leaped for it. She listened, with a puzzled look, then handed it to me. At first there was silence, then a hoarse croak, something fighting to sound like a voice.

'Who's this? Nicola? Is it you?'

She choked out a few incoherent words.

'Where are you?'

She was at the Theodore. She wasn't well. She didn't know how to get home. I was on my feet, reaching for the car keys, when Colette came on the line.

'Helen?' she chirped. 'Hello there! How's your day been? Now, Nicky's had a reaction to the vitamin C. She's a tiny bit shaky—but don't worry—everything's fine. Listen, though—we're just about to close for the day.'

Something in me exploded. 'How long has she been in this state?' I shouted. 'Why haven't you called me before this? It's peak hour. The roads are jam-packed. It'll take me an hour to drive into the city!'

Three faces stared up at me from the couch.

'Now Helen, don't get excited,' said Colette. 'Nicky's here beside me. She's smiling. She wants me to tell you she's quite all right.'

'What sort of an outfit is this?' I said shrilly. 'Surely you don't think you can just shove her into a taxi, in this state? Tell me how you think we're going to get her home.'

A muffled confab took place just out of my hearing.

'Good news,' cried Colette. 'Professor Theodore lives out your way. He'll drive her home. They should be there in half an hour.'

I banged down the phone. 'He's coming here. That wanker who runs the clinic. He's driving her home.'

'Who? Who? Who?' said Bessie.

'Let's be ready for him,' said Gab. 'You fix Nicola's room and we'll clear up out here.'

I took Bessie by the hand and dragged her protesting to the gap in the fence. 'I might have to be very rude to someone,' I said. 'I don't want you to hear it.'

Then I skidded into my office and dialled the number of a lawyer I knew. She was still at her desk.

'Listen. I need to make a complaint about a shady alternative health clinic. What's the government body to approach?'

'That would be the Health Services Commission, I believe,' she replied calmly. 'What's going on?'

'I need to make some threatening noises and I

don't want them to sound hollow.'

Half an hour passed; an hour. I kept running out the front door and looking up and down the street. No sign of them. By seven I was in a panic. I found the clinic's card and called the number. The answering machine was on: the office was closed until Monday. In the bottom corner of the card was a mobile number. I dialled it. A man answered.

'I'm looking for my friend Nicola, a patient at the Theodore Institute,' I said. 'Someone's driving her home and I'm worried about her—do you have any idea where she is?'

'Yes, Nicola's with me,' said the man. 'We're just turning into Mount Alexander Road.'

'Is she all right?'

'She's fine. We should be at your place in about ten minutes.'

'Are you Professor Theodore?'

'I am.'

'I need to talk to you very seriously,' I said, 'about Nicola's treatment.'

'Well,' he said. 'Whatever it is you want to say, you'd better say it right now.'

I could hear the rush of traffic. 'I'm not going to

have this conversation with you on a mobile, while you're driving my friend in your car.'

'Last chance, I'm afraid,' he said languidly. 'I'm going overseas first thing tomorrow morning.'

What? He was off again? My hands began to shake.

'When you get her to my house,' I said, 'I think you'd better come in.'

The line went dead.

Iris stepped out of the bathroom, smelling fresh and lemony. Her crazy curls were tied back with a rag of bright cotton. She smiled at me, and plumped up the couch cushions. Gab came into the room in a clean T-shirt.

'All right, Helen,' he said. He had dark brown eyes set in deep sockets. 'Ready to rock.'

I wanted to dissolve in sobs of gratitude. They were young, they were sane, and they were in my corner.

~

Nicola came through the screen door first. A man in a suit was trailing behind her. She stumbled down the hall towards her room with both hands out and her teeth bared, panting, fighting to speak.

'Water. Gimme some water. And one o' those— one o' those—'

'You want morphine?'

She lurched to her bed. Her knees buckled and she fell sideways on to it.

The man hovered close to the front door, as if ready to bolt. I ran to the kitchen for water and back to her room. Her teeth were chattering, she was streaming sweat. I worked the sodden clothes and shoes off her. She was grunting in pain, gasping with it; but on her poor face, as she seized the glass of water and gulped down the pill, she was still managing to stretch from ear to ear that frightful, agonised, social smile.

I took the glass and settled her back against the pillows. She looked up at me anxiously in the half dark, trying to speak.

'Now I'm going to sort out that arsehole,' I said. I turned and made for the door.

'Hel,' she croaked after me. 'Hel. He hasn't done anything wrong.'

~

Gab and Iris had ushered the professor into the big back room and established him in an armchair. He was leaning back with his knees apart and his hands spread on the armrests. We inspected each other with narrow eyes. I had pictured someone glamorous, a sun-tanned globe-trotter in a hemp jacket, but in his tight suit and slip-on shoes he looked more like a salesman or a preacher, balding, fading, but ready to brazen it out.

Iris brought a tray and laid it on the low table between us. China and glass clinked in the awkward silence.

'I'm afraid I can only stay a minute,' said the professor in a distant tone, taking a sip of tea. 'I'm off to a conference in Mexico, early in the morning.'

'How come you're always leaving town?' I burst out. 'And why did you say on the phone just now that she was fine? She's beyond speech, she's in pain, she's desperate—is that what you call fine?'

From the corner of my eye I saw Gab drop his face and look at his hands. I grabbed a glass of water and swigged it.

'Anyone with experience of the treatments,' said the professor, 'would know that such reactions are...fleeting.'

'I have experience. I've been picking up the pieces for the past fortnight. I need you to tell me why you keep brutalising her like this.'

He looked at me levelly. 'Many cancer treatments can look "brutal" to the untrained observer,' he said.

'Yes but what's it all based on? What's the evidence that vitamin C works? And why aren't there any properly qualified staff supervising it?'

He looked surprised. 'Our staff are perfectly qualified to administer the treatments. One of them's a specialist.'

I switched tack again and blundered on. 'Why don't you tell the truth to people? She thinks her cancer's going to get better. You must know it's not.'

'We don't offer our patients prognoses,' said the professor, setting his cup in its saucer.

'Well that's a lie,' I said. 'I looked in her file. It said right there, in big fat letters, *terminal.* How can you lead people on like this? It's shameful. Shame on you.'

Iris leaned forward and laid her hand on my knee. I tried to control myself, but when the professor raised an ironic eyebrow I began to bluster.

'You won't get away with it this time, because I'm going to report you.'

'And who,' he drawled, tilting his head, 'were you thinking of reporting me *to*?'

I slapped down my pathetic ace. 'To the Health Services Commission.'

He gave a casual little hiccup of laughter. 'And uhm—what exactly, might I ask, are you going to "report"?'

I was no use to anyone in this state, poisoned and choking with rage. Hot-faced, I sat back in my chair.

Gab took a deep breath. 'Look, Professor Theodore,' he said in his mild, reasonable voice. 'Both Iris and I are if anything rather in favour of alternative treatments. But we're concerned by the state Nicola comes home in. And we're wondering if you could explain to us the scientific basis for the treatments your clinic offers, specially the vitamin C. We'd like to look into it. Maybe get on to the internet and read up on it. Can you give us any pointers?'

As the professor began to lay out his authorities, I got up and stumped out across the back veranda. I picked my way between the vegetable rows and put my head through the gap in the fence. The next-door yard was empty. They must be inside having their tea. Kids' junk was strewn about on the dry grass. A pink ballet shoe lay on the rubber bed of the trampoline. The swing dangled from a fig tree branch. One of the guinea pigs bustled across the asphalt near the barbecue with a long blade of grass poking out of its mouth. Dully I looked at its pop eyes, its thick neck and hulking shoulders. What were guinea pigs for? They were just lumps with fur on them. In Peru people roasted and ate them, but here they looked prehistoric, left behind by evolution, and pointlessly busy, with all that moronic nibbling and chewing and scuttling and mating. A waste of space and energy.

What was the matter with me? How could I hate a creature for leading its tiny, inoffensive life in the corner of somebody's yard?

Why should a dog, a horse, a rat have life,
And thou no breath at all?

~

I slunk into the kitchen just in time to see the professor's back retreating down the hall. I caught up with him as he passed the closed door of Nicola's room. There he turned to me and said, 'Don't you want to check if she'd like to see me, before I leave?' Even in the dark hall I saw his expression: he was scoring a point, suggesting I had been remiss. I opened her door and tiptoed in.

She was awake, but terribly white and groggy.

'Professor Theodore's off now. Want him to pop in and see you before he goes?'

'I'm fine,' she said in a faint, slurred voice. 'Tell him I'm fine. And Hel—would you thank him? Say thank you very much.'

Somehow I got myself out the door. He was standing there waiting, his features arranged in a configuration of professional solicitude. I repeated her words. He nodded, and strode off towards his car. As he clicked the front gate shut behind him, he tossed a parting remark over his shoulder.

'Much better weather we've been having this week, isn't it.'

9

NICOLA slept, or we assumed she was sleeping, for she did not stir from her room. Iris and I lay on the couches in our pyjamas, drinking soda water, clipping and painting our toenails, and blankly watching TV, while Gab ransacked the internet. Towards eleven he emerged. He was the sort of man who could stretch his spine and make it crackle all the way down.

'I can't find anything substantial to validate the vitamin C,' he said. 'Everyone got very excited about it in the sixties. But then they hit it with proper randomised trials. Double-blind, placebo-controlled. And it all went pretty much pear-shaped. Theodore mentioned what he said was an important paper by some guy called Webster.'

'A paper?' said Iris. 'What—just the one?'

'Well I found the guy, but all the magazines that run his research are super alternative. Some of them seem to be owned by him. But one thing I did find out about Theodore—he's a vet.'

He threw himself on to the couch and laid his head on Iris's lap.

'A "research scientist", he calls himself,' he added.

We sprawled there in a complicated silence.

'I've been thinking,' said Iris, 'about why Helen got so angry.'

Oh God. I was going to have to account for myself. I sat up. 'I'm so sorry. I lost it. It's the worst thing about me—I'm an angry person. Anger's my default mode.'

Gab uttered a muffled laugh, and looked up at Iris. Her cheeks had gone pink. She glanced over her shoulder towards the hall door and lowered her voice.

'You have to understand,' she said, 'that I love Nicola very much. She's been a huge figure for me, ever since I was a child. But I've never been so angry in my life as I was when she came to stay at my place.

I really thought I was going to have to kill her myself, and save the cancer the trouble.'

'I knew she was with you too long,' I said. 'I used to spend hours composing diplomatic emails: "Don't you think you should rent yourself a little place of your own in Elizabeth Bay? Get out of Iris's hair?" And she'd answer in that high-handed tone— "Darling, Iris adores me. She loves having me there."'

We all laughed, painfully.

'She's been there since April,' said Iris. 'And she's got no plans to leave. Melbourne's just a holiday. All her gear's still piled in my front hall.'

'It's a one-bedroom flat,' said Gab, without rancour. 'Iris gave Nicola the bed. We've been sleeping on the living room floor.'

'Want to hear my theory?' said Iris. 'There's a lot of horribleness that Nicola refuses to countenance. But it won't just go away. It can't, because it exists. So somebody else has to sort of live it. It's in the air around her. Like static. I felt it when she walked into the house tonight. It was like I suddenly had a temperature. My heart rate went up.'

I stared at her. 'You mean it's not just me?'

'No way. I know exactly what you're feeling. It's

terrible. It's like getting a madness injection.'

'I get prickling,' I said, 'in the backs of my hands.'

'She's cast us as the carriers of all the bad stuff—and somehow we've let her. She sails about with that ghastly smile on her face, telling everyone she's going to be better by the middle of next week, and meanwhile we're trawling along the bottom picking up all the anguish and rage that she's thrown overboard.'

'Can people do that?' said Gab, propping himself on his elbows.

'Remember, Gab?' said Iris. 'The first time she had the vitamin C? She was catatonic—like tonight—but they turfed her out and she had to drive herself home. Across the Harbour Bridge at peak hour. I couldn't believe it. I was insane with rage. I wanted to go straight over to that clinic and hurl a grenade through their front window. But the next morning she was so offhand about it that I ended up thinking I must have over-reacted. She patronised me. I felt a fool.'

'It was pretty deflating,' said Gab.

'That's what she does here,' I said. 'She almost makes fun of me.'

They looked at me. Iris's lips were quivering.

'I've hardly had a night's sleep since she arrived,' I said. 'I shop, I cook, I clean. I field her unwanted phone calls. I'm a hand-maiden. A washer-woman. I lump her fucking mattress around and prop it in the sun. And all that's fine—it really is—I'd do anything for her. But then last week she made it abundantly clear to me that she "doesn't need a nurse".'

We had to press our faces into the cushions to stifle our laughter. Gab soon sobered up, but Iris and I went on and on, in fits that would not stop. He sat patiently by, with his hand resting on the back of her neck, and watched us gasp and groan.

~

I had always thought that sorrow was the most exhausting of the emotions. Now I knew that it was anger. I lay galvanised on my bed for the rest of the night, seething and staring into the dark. Whenever I nodded off for a moment, the professor with his watery eyes and high colour slouched in and stood by the bed, grinning like a defrocked priest.

At last the morning slid between the slats of the

venetian blind. In the kitchen I filled the kettle and tore open the newspaper. Nicola came shuffling along the hall. Her head was high, the eyebrows arched, the smile huge and riveted on. She greeted me tunefully.

'Goooood morning, darling friend!'

'Don't speak to me, Nicola,' I muttered, turning away to the bench. 'I can't even look at you, I'm so livid.'

'Oo-wah.' she trilled, in a mocking girlish treble.

'And don't give me that oo-wah shit. Don't you dare.' Sweat broke out under my pyjama top. I glanced down at my chest and saw the ugly flush rising.

She paused in the doorway in her nightie, holding the red wool shawl round her like a peasant.

'What's wrong, Hel?'

The crimson of her shawl was leaking into the air around her, staining it.

'There's something I would like to know,' I said. 'When are you going to get real?'

Her mouth fell open. 'What do you mean?'

'Don't act dumb. I nurse you, I wait on you hand and foot, and then you turn around and laugh at me. You laughed at me.'

'When? What are you talking about?'

'At Peggy's. You laughed at me for being scared at night. You made a joke of it. *Poor old Hel.*'

'Oh, that?' she said. 'A week ago.' She put out one hand to me, palm up, and drew in her chin. Her eyebrows formed an inverted V of patronising concern. 'I'm so sorry, darling. I had no idea I'd offended you.'

She tilted her head, stretched her lips, and there it was again, plastered across her face like latex—the smile.

The last of my self-control gave way.

'Get that grin off your face. Get it off, or I'll wipe it off for you.'

It faded of its own accord. She took two steps backwards, gaping at me. 'Why are you so angry?'

'This house is full of anger! Can't you feel it? The rooms are stuffed with it. And a lot of it's got to be yours.'

Her mouth was half open, her cheeks hollow. Everything I looked at was blood-coloured. I couldn't stop now.

'Everyone's angry, everyone's scared,' I shouted. 'You're angry and scared. But you won't admit it. You want to keep up this masquerade, so you dump your

137

shit on me. I'm sick with it. I can't breathe.'

She cowered against the arm of the couch.

'That creep who brought you back here last night. Can't you see what a quack he is? He's taking you for a huge ride.'

'Darling,' she stammered. 'He's helping me. They're the only ones who are helping me.'

'Oh, they're not helping you. That airhead Colette, the sappy fat guy. And the famous specialist. They're so creepy and repulsive. Why won't they do anything about your pain? They don't even seem to notice that you're suffering.'

'Suffering?' she said. 'Helen, there's a woman in there with only one leg.'

'What about yesterday? They would have shoved you into a taxi if I hadn't kicked up a stink. They know what the vitamin C does to you—why wasn't anyone monitoring you?'

'One of the other patients was,' said Nicola. 'She's a nurse. She was keeping an eye on me.'

'And they charge you two grand a week for this? Leaving it to another patient to look after you?'

She bridled. 'Janine's not just any old nurse. She's an intensive care nurse.'

Where was this rage stored in me? It gushed up like nausea.

'Can't you use your brains? Look what they're doing. Their treatments are bullshit, Nicola. They're ripping you off. They can't cure cancer.'

'They can so.' She raised her chin and glared at me. 'They can.'

'If you can prove to me that intravenous vitamin C cures cancer,' I said, 'I'll give that sleaze-bag professor a million bucks. Show me the evidence.'

'There was a man up in Grafton,' she said. 'A sculptor. He got better.'

'That's not evidence. That's an anecdote.'

'There's plenty more,' she said. 'Pages and pages of it. I didn't bring it but I've got it at home.'

'Yeah right,' I said savagely, 'and it must be true, because you got it off their website.'

My heart was beating so hard that black spots danced at the edge of my vision. Against the red shawl Nicola's face had turned grey and sagged out of shape. Behind her, Iris appeared at the hall door. She paused on the threshold in her flannel pyjamas, a light presence, her arms folded across her chest. Shame choked me: I was a bully, caught in the act.

'I can't go on with this,' I said, in a high voice. 'I can't stand the falseness. It's making me sick. I'm going off my head.'

Nicola's shoulders slumped. Her neck came forward and her head bowed. Iris padded forward into the room. She sat on the arm of the couch beside Nicola, put one arm round her shoulders, then turned her face up to me and mouthed with exaggerated lip movements, 'Keep. Going.'

Shocked, I stared at her. She was holding Nicola upright, but nodding at me, her eyes clear and steady, her mouth in a straight, determined line.

I took a couple of big gulps of air, and drove on.

'After that professor went home, Nicola,' I said, 'I wanted to come into your room and say to you, Wake up.'

'I was awake,' she whispered.

'I wanted to say this. You're using that bloody clinic to distract yourself.'

Like an old, tired dog she heaved up her head. 'Don't say it, Hel.'

'From what you have to do.'

She raised one palm. 'Don't tell me.'

'You've got to get ready.'

Her head drooped lower. Iris took hold of her in both arms. Nicola gave in, and let her head tip sideways into the curve of the girl's shoulder. I could see her face distorting, her mouth clenching, the tears starting to run. The fight drained out of me. My limbs felt chalky and weak.

'We can't find you any more,' I said. 'We miss you. Where have you gone?'

She let out a thick sob.

'We can't bear what you're going through,' I said. 'We can't bear to lose you. We want to look after you. You're so dear to us. But you crack hardy. You hold us away. We can't get to you. You fight us off. And you make us feel silly for getting upset.'

She let Iris support her head, while tears swarmed out of her eyes and dripped off her cheeks. Soon the breast of the girl's pyjama jacket was darkly soaked. Iris kept her grip, holding on with both arms, saying nothing, but every few seconds looking up at me and nodding, nodding.

'You wear us out, when you keep on being stoical,' I said. 'It's like a horrible mask. We want to smash it. We want to find you.'

'We can't bear the smile, darling,' said Iris gently.

'You don't have to smile.'

Nicola wept on, in her niece's embrace. Gab came to the door, looked in, and crept away. But Iris held my gaze without a flicker, her sober face tilted up towards the bench behind which I stood wringing the dry dishcloth in both hands.

In a little while Nicola stopped crying. She took a few quivering breaths, and freed herself from Iris's arms. Iris reached for a clean tea towel and handed it to her; she dabbed at her eyes, folded it, and laid it on the bench.

Then, in a hoarse voice, she said, 'But see all my life I've never wanted to bore people with the way I feel.'

We were silent.

'No one wants to know about it, if I'm sad or frightened.'

Again we said nothing.

'I've learnt,' she went on, 'to shut up. And present an optimistic face.'

She got off the couch arm and stood in her cotton nightie in the middle of the room. Light from the high window blurred her white hair. The shawl hung like two red curtains from her bony shoulders.

'Anyway,' she said. 'That's what life has taught me.'

Iris leaned back against the couch and surveyed her with a soft face.

'Bullshit, darling,' she said. 'I'm sorry, but that is so not the way to live.'

For a moment no one moved, or spoke.

'You think your life's been wasted,' I said.

'It has.'

'I would like to dispute that.'

'So would I,' said Iris.

'Why do people love you?' I said.

Nicola stood in the patch of light, wearing an almost comical expression of surprise.

'You don't suppose it could be because of your character?' I said. 'Like for example what a faithful friend you are? Who has never been known to bear a grudge?'

She took a breath to make little of it, but I spoke over her.

'Or your bottomless generosity? The way everything you touch becomes beautiful?'

'What about how funny you are?' said Iris, warming to it.

'And those play-readings we used to have, that were your idea? When we did *She Stoops to Conquer* and *The Seagull?*'

'All the work you do for people and never ask for payment? Reading their novels—draft after draft? Rewriting whole plays?'

'Yes, and the way you listen when people talk? You even remember the details. When people are with you they feel free. Don't you know that? You think this is waste?'

There was another long silence.

Iris crossed the room to the windows, and raised the blinds. Rectangles of sunlight fell across the table. I opened the back door. Everything out there lay serene. The air that touched the cheek was fresh. Sun was warming the flat sides of things, the old brick paving. The fly curtain sprinkled its beads against the door frame, and once more hung motionless.

'I wish I still smoked,' said Nicola. 'I'd go out on that veranda and I'd bloody well roll myself one.'

She brushed through the beaded strands. Iris followed her.

The kettle boiled and I brought the tray.

We sat on the back step in a line, and drank our tea. Someone said, 'Isn't it a lovely morning!' And someone said, 'Will we buy some fish for dinner?' Nicola rested her shoulder against mine. We looked each other in the eyes and away again, open and free. It was like being submerged to our chins in calm water. Our limbs were weightless, and so were our hearts. I looked at the clock. It was only half past eight.

10

RAVAGED she might have been, but Nicola scrubbed up like a dream. All it took was an afternoon of dozing behind the faintly tapping wooden blind, then a shallow bath, a subtle whisk of makeup, and a morphine capsule gulped on the wing: by eight that evening she was manoeuvring her sore body into the car beside me, grunting with discomfort, but scarved and perfumed, as game as a duchess in exile. How long could this truce last? I wanted to trust it. Gaily we sped across the river to South Melbourne, where a young German magician whose show I had promised to review was to perform at a weird little bar called the Butterfly Club.

We carried our drinks into the high-ceilinged

side room where the show would soon begin, and took the two seats I had bagged in the front row, only a couple of feet from the magician's austere baize-covered table. It was exciting to be out together, to sit there in the best chairs while a dozen strangers filed in behind us and settled whispering and clinking in the half dark.

The magician in his loose old pin-striped suit entered the room without fanfare, sliding in at the back and approaching the table on soft shoes, so that his presence washed through the room like a wave. Everyone sat forward. He set down his suitcase and clicked open its brass hasps. Smiling at us, he took out of it a metal cup, a white ball the size of an apricot stone, and a short, dark wand tipped with brass at either end. He placed them on the green cloth.

He avoided my eye, but looked straight at Nicola.

'The most beautiful things,' he remarked to her in a German-tinged drawl, 'happen secretly and privately.'

A broad, eager grin spread across her face. She was his. He had chosen her; he would use her.

He pushed back his cuffs and picked up between thumb and forefinger the tiny white ball.

'There are many ways,' he said to Nicola, 'to make a thing disappear. Do you want me to show you the fast way or the slow way?'

She smiled, and nodded many times, but did not reply. He twinkled his handsome dark eyes at her, and pursed his lips; then his hands executed a sinuous flurry. The white ball darted up the cuff of his left sleeve and reappeared two beats later on his right palm. On the baize table he covered the ball with the metal cup, tapped the cup with his wand, and made a magic twirl. When he raised the cup, the white ball had vanished into the ether. Next time he raised the cup, there it was again—but it was red. He clapped the cup down over it.

'Red or white?'

'White?' said Nicola.

We all sat forward. He raised the cup. The red ball had quadrupled in size and turned into a lemon.

People rocked back in shouts of laughter. Nicola bit her bottom lip and rounded her eyes at me.

He worked on us for twenty rapt minutes that

passed like seconds, caressing our ears with a patter full of charming grammatical mistakes. He sprayed a deck of cards through space, in an arc as smooth as water. He made coins change denomination in mid-air. He asked a man to pick a card from his pack, then with both hands flung the entire deck to the sky. It slammed against the ceiling. We craned up. Cards showered down on our heads and shoulders. Only one stuck to the high plaster.

'Have you ever saw this card before?'

'It's my card!' cried the man.

Next the magician produced from his suitcase two small, dark red globular objects that he identified as 'genetically modified Dutch tomatoes'. Again he turned to Nicola.

'Your hand, Madame?'

She offered it. He turned it palm up and placed on it the two red globes.

'Please, Madame, if you would squeeze? Squeeze as hard as you are able.'

Nicola squeezed. She squeezed until her hand trembled. Then she opened it. On her palm lay three Dutch tomatoes.

Some women behind us let out a shriek. Men

were stamping their feet. Nicola held the red things out to him. He took them from her tenderly, with a bow. She flashed her shining face at me. The room hushed.

Then the magician drew from his little suitcase a length of soft, pearl-white cord. He showed it to us: it was about a metre long, and quite limp. He stepped back against the wall, and without a word began to do things with the cord that were not possible. It had a life and will of its own: he was its servant, its guardian. It broke in two, in three and four. It tied itself in and out of knots which glided this way and that. It grew long, it grew short. It disintegrated—Nicola gasped and gripped my arm—and then it comforted us by turning back into a perfect white O that hung free from his small, muscular hands.

On a tide of joy he surfed out of the room, waving. The door clicked shut behind him. We all stayed in our seats. It was unbearable that he had left us. In the sudden silence I heard Nicola pull in a quivering line of breath. Her spine was starting to sag forward: she was flagging.

We flew home along King Street, just as the haunts of drunken footballers and identical blondes were opening their doors for the night's business. We were quiet, thinking about what we had seen. Then, as we passed the North Melbourne pool, she spoke.

'Hel, which bits did you believe?'

'All of it. There must be an explanation for everything he did. But I don't want to know what it was.'

'Which was your favourite bit?'

'Oh, the white cord,' I said. 'The cord, no contest. That was transcendental.'

I took the green arrow into Macaulay Road.

'What did those Dutch tomatoes feel like?' I asked.

'Spongy. Like foam.'

'How on earth did he make the right card stick to the ceiling? And the way he turned that ball into a lemon.'

'I loved all of it,' she said. 'But Hel. My absolute best bit was at the very start, when he looked right at me and said, "There are many ways to make a thing disappear".'

I said nothing. She kept her eyes down. I heard her stifle a gasp of pain as the car thumped over the railway tracks and crossed the Moonee Ponds Creek in the dark.

~

On Sunday, trying to sleep in, she delayed taking a pill, and the pain got on top of her. By lunchtime it had sunk its claws into her left arm and shoulder. She fought it back with the morphine, but the afternoon was long and frightening. Iris spent more than an hour in the spare room with her, and emerged in tears.

'She won't come home. She says there's no point bolting after two weeks if the treatment's based on three. She says she wants to keep faith with Professor Theodore.'

Gab came in from the garden, and they packed their bags in sombre silence. At dusk I drove them to the airport.

'I feel we're abandoning you,' said Iris at the check-in.

'Let's see how we go,' I said.

'Can you keep doing this?'

'I think so.'

'Are you sure?'

'No. But I want to try. Only six more sleeps. Where's she going to live, when she comes back to Sydney?'

'My place, I guess,' said Iris.

'It's gone way beyond that, Iris. You're a teacher, for God's sake. You can't hold down a job and handle this as well. She needs a place of her own, but within reach of people who can take it in turns. It's time for your mother to step in.'

Iris made a flinching grimace. 'Nicola wouldn't hack that,' she said. 'She'd take it as interference— from Mum, or from anybody.'

'Let her. She's got to have steady, relentless looking-after now, whether she wants it or not. Couldn't your mum rent her some nice sunny little flat in Elizabeth Bay?'

Iris had gone pale. 'She'd arc up. Mum's life wouldn't be worth living. And leases are long.'

'One foolproof way to get out of a lease,' I said tartly, 'would be to die.'

The girl's eyes filled with tears. She dashed them away. Gab strode towards us across the ocean of shiny tiles. He shook my hand and hugged me.

'Goodbye,' said Iris. 'Goodbye, Helen. We're friends now, aren't we.'

'We've got to be,' I said. 'I'll miss you. You're a pair of troupers.'

In two days I had come to depend on their company: Gab's good-natured calm, Iris's reedy voice and droll expressions. When she stooped to kiss me, I caught a whiff of her soap. The tarry scent of it got under my guard. I hated seeing their two tall figures, smooth-headed and curly, pass through security and disappear.

In the car I was lonely and scared. I let out a couple of dry sobs. On either side of the freeway, the lights of new industrial parks were flicking on. I wound the window down and punched the radio button. Cat Empire: 'Nights Like These'. Once I had overheard a spiteful girl dismiss that band as just a bunch of private schoolboys: what would they know about the end of everything? But the clattering percussion. Those horns, the creamy thread of trumpet. I cranked it up and began to yell the words. *I'm alive, I'm alive, I'm alive, I'm alive, I'm aliiiiiiiive...*

Nicola had fallen asleep, but when I looked round her door she stirred. The bed was dank with sweat, the pillow a packed lump. I worked to make things right. I brought her a juice and a clean nightie and another pill.

'Tomorrow we'll get stronger morphine,' I said. 'We'll go back to Dr Caplan.'

~

Monday was my birthday. At breakfast Nicola showered me with gifts large and small that she had secretly arranged for Iris and Gab to buy in the city during the weekend. Her *pièce de résistance* was a splendid juicer. She sallied forth that morning in high good humour, chattering keenly, as we drove to Dr Caplan's rooms, about the birthday dinner Mitch and Eva had planned for me that evening.

When we were called into the surgery I dived for the seat near the door, and Nicola shuffled to the patient's chair beside the doctor at her desk.

'I think I need stronger morphine,' she announced, with a smile so sheepish it made her look like a simpleton.

Dr Caplan stared at her, incredulous, almost laughing. Her eyes shone with a furious intelligence.

I was scared of her. I wanted to shout *Please help me.*

'Who's co-ordinating your treatment?' she snapped. 'Who's handling your pain?'

She twisted on her swivel chair, twining her bare, skinny legs around each other under the desk.

'What do you think—what's your name? Helen?' She flung a scornful look at me over her grey linen shoulder. 'How are you experiencing all this?'

I floundered. 'Nicola doesn't like to hear me say it,' I said. 'But they're negligent. They don't have proper supervision. They—'

She cut across me and turned back to Nicola. 'Who referred you to them?'

'My GP in Sydney,' said Nicola. Her head was hanging forward like a crone's. 'He specialises in cancer.'

The doctor lowered her face so she could look Nicola in the eye.

'Most people with an illness like yours,' she said, articulating with textbook crispness, 'and who went interstate for treatment, would take with them a letter from their oncologist. A documentation of their condition and the treatments they've already had. I can't tell what your cancer's doing. You need to go to an oncologist here. And you need someone to put proper pain-management in place.'

She pulled a pad towards her and drove her pen across it.

'I'm sending you straight to this oncologist,' she said. 'His name's John Maloney. I'm going to call him and tell him you're coming. You're to make an appointment. Today. Is that clear?'

Again she raked me with a look. It stung me to be included in her contempt. I almost burst into a whine: *It's not my fault! You don't understand what I'm up against.*

She tapped out a script for stronger morphine and handed it to Nicola. We walked back to the Theodore Institute with our tails between our legs, and I set off again for the Epworth.

~

At five o'clock Nicola slid through the front door and straight into her room. Half an hour later she limped out to the kitchen, where I was playing with my new juicer. She had the shudders again, she said, and the pain in her arm was bad. In a quiet, unstrained voice she asked me for help.

In her room I closed the blind and switched on the heater. She lay down groaning and shivering. I brought her a glass of water and she swallowed one of the new morphine capsules. She turned on to her side.

'My shoulder's killing me. And it was probably just the steam, but this morning when I was getting out of the shower I couldn't catch my breath.'

'Did you call the oncologist?'

'Yep,' she said. 'Seeing him Wednesday morning. The Theodore people have heard of him. Colette says he can get a bit snaky.'

I lay down behind her, with my whole front against her back, while she waited for the morphine. Cold shudders rippled down her torso and along her limbs.

'I don't think I'll do the vitamin C any more,' she murmured. 'It's too hard. I'm too weak for it, at the moment.'

This was what I had been fighting for, but my heart began to ache.

'Hel,' she said, after a long time. 'Thanks for letting me stay.'

'My house is your house.'

'I knew I was almost out of energy. It was all I could do to get to you.'

'Go to sleep, now.'

'And thanks for yelling at me in the kitchen. It was brave.'

'Brave? I don't know how you can forgive me. I monstered you.'

'Yeah, but it worked.'

A tremor of laughter ran through her.

'When I was having a nap afterwards,' she said, 'I had a really vivid dream. There was this cute puppy, like a cartoon dog, with floppy sweet little ears.' Her voice softened. 'And as I looked at it, a great big pair of scissors appeared and went *snip! snip!* Cut off both its ears.'

Aghast, I stared at the nape of her neck.

She made a blurry sound, half laugh half grunt. 'It's good, darling. Cutting off all that childish crap.'

We lay in the dimmed room like two felled logs. I could feel her torso loosening, giving in.

'Hel,' she whispered. 'I don't think I'll make it to the dinner. You go. Have a drink for me. Happy birthday, ol' bean ol' pea.'

~

Light rain was falling. I picked my way through the vegetables to the gap in the fence and up the yard. The house next door was in turmoil. Some cousins with their three children had come for the meal. The fathers were locked in conference about the roasting lamb, the mothers were laughing on the couch with their heads together, and the toddlers, their hair standing on end like dandelion fluff, were thundering among the furniture beating each other with rolled-up newspapers. Bessie was lost in a fit of melodramatic weeping for which no one could find a motive. Her cousin Frank, a thoughtful child to whom she was passionately devoted, loitered just outside the room, disconcerted, bored and patient.

'Come on, Bessie Boop, you've got to stop crying,' I said.

She heard the mechanical note in my protest and redoubled her howls.

'You must stop,' I said pointlessly. 'Stop now.'

I carried her front to front into the laundry where between her heaves and gasps I managed to insert a question about a new shelf her father had built there. Instantly she snapped out of it, and engaged me in a cheerful discussion of how I might have exactly such a shelf installed in my laundry. We went out to the back veranda, sat on its edge with our feet on the steps, and watched the drizzle.

Frank wormed in between us. They looked at each other fondly. Soon they invited me to play a game they had invented called Going to Lands.

'How about we go to Shoeland?' said Frank.

'In Shoeland,' Bessie explained to me, 'everything has to have a shoe on it. Water has a shoe on it.'

'Air has a shoe on it.'

'A roof has a shoe on it.'

'Even poo,' said Frank, 'has a tiny shoe on it.'

Thus we comforted and entertained ourselves. The rain kept gently falling. Mitch brought me a glass of sparkling shiraz. Soon the dinner was on the table. All was orderly and festive. There were sixty-four candles. The effort to blow them out made my head spin.

Every half-hour I ran home to check on Nicola. The first few times she was asleep. Then I found her sitting on the edge of her bed in the dark, eyes closed, spine bowed, hands folded in her lap. Her loneliness pierced me.

'What can I bring you, old girl?'

'In all the world,' she said in a slurred voice, 'I most would love a glass of orange juice.'

I squeezed the last two fruits we had, and brought her the foaming glass. She drank it sip by sip.

'That,' she whispered, 'was the freshest, most delicious orange juice I've ever drunk in my life.'

I tucked her back into bed, and she subsided with a sigh.

When at ten o'clock I came home for good, I stood outside her door for a long time and listened to her slow, snoring breaths. One day soon they would stop. Would I be with her when she went? I was her friend, yes, and I loved her, but I was a recent friend: I had known her for only fifteen years. Surely her dearest, her oldest friends were Sydney people. In a couple of days, when her three weeks with me were over, she would fly home to them, and to her family: they would take over, and I would go back to my role as *darling Hel in Melbourne*, the practical type with a handy authoritarian streak, who had work to do and a ticket to Vienna in December.

11

ON TUESDAY morning, to escape the attentions of Bessie, I planned to take my laptop to the State Library and knock over the magician review there. Nicola and I could catch the same train to the city.

The station was a seven-minute walk from my house, twenty if you had cancer. It was still lightly raining. I dug out my two umbrellas. As I pulled the front door shut behind us, I glanced at Nicola's feet. On them was her usual pair of Chinese slippers made of thin black cotton fabric.

'Hey, dingdong,' I said. 'Notice water falling from the sky? You can't wear those.'

'Don't be silly, darling. I'll be fine.'

'Nicola. The street is full of puddles. You'll have

wet feet all day. You'll catch cold.'

'But I haven't brought anything else.' She made as if to step out on to the darkened bricks.

'Put on your Dunlop Volleys.'

'They wore out,' she said. 'I went to Gowing's for a new pair, but they don't make the originals any more. I refuse to buy those ugly modern ones.'

She came to me with no proper shoes. The backs of my hands set up their treacherous prickling. The rain continued to fall, hitting the mulch with soft, sparse pats. I closed my eyes and rapped out an order.

'You must go out at lunchtime today and get yourself some runners. Go to Sam Bear, or Target in Bourke Street. I don't care if they're original or retro or whatever the fuck they are—you've got to have a decent pair of wet weather shoes.'

'All right, Matron,' she said, humbly. Then she sparked up. 'I know. We can drive to the station.'

'Yes,' I said, 'but there's only one-hour parking. I'll drive you to the station, and come back here and leave the car, then I'll catch the next train.'

'Oh, but that's such a nuisance for you, darling.'

'There's no choice,' I said. 'Hop in.'

Outside Newmarket station I sat behind the wheel and watched her shuffle doggedly up the ramp in her inadequate footwear. I was free now till late afternoon. The State Library seemed a thousand miles away. How could I drag myself that far? I parked the car and took the laptop into the cafe on the corner. I had never written anything in a cafe and I wasn't going to start now. My heart was full of holes. Everything strong and purposeful was draining out of me. When my coffee came I could hardly lift the cup. I drove home. My desk was buried under sliding heaps of unread and unanswered mail. I had lost control of my life. I laid the laptop down and began drearily to sort things into some sort of order.

Deep in the pile I found a scrap of paper bearing the scribbled words *Health Services Commission*. A worm of energy stirred in me. I looked it up in the phone book and called the number. A woman answered. I told her I wanted to make a complaint about an alternative cancer clinic that I believed was a fraud.

'Are you the patient?' she asked.

'No. I'm the patient's friend.'

'Then I'm afraid there's nothing we can do for

you,' she said, in a kind but finalising tone. 'We can only take complaints from people who've undergone treatment.'

'Wait. Wait,' I said. 'I can understand that—but I don't imagine I'd be the only person objecting to this joint. Maybe you could take down what I witnessed, and use it as corroboration for other complaints.'

'No, I don't think so,' she said.

'Is there any other government body I could approach?'

'Not that I know of.'

'Well—what am I supposed to do, then?'

'What's the name of the place?' she said, humouring me.

'The Theodore Institute.'

An electric silence. Then she said, in a voice whose sudden aliveness she could not conceal, 'Would you hold the line a moment?'

I waited. When she came back she was fully present.

'Yes, we would like to hear what you've got to say. I'm going to give you the name of an investigator. You should call him and make an appointment.'

He was driving on the freeway when I reached his mobile. He pulled over immediately. He sounded like a cop. I told him the story and he listened without a single interruption.

The Theodore Institute, he said, had been under investigation for some time. It was acceptable for me to make a complaint without Nicola's permission, as long as I myself had seen who administered the treatments.

'Will your friend speak to me?'

'No way. She thinks they're going to save her life. I'm doing this behind her back.'

'I could come to your house next week. Would you be prepared to talk on tape?'

'Is the Pope a Catholic?'

He laughed. Was that the roar of freeway traffic, or the distant hoof-beats of the cavalry?

~

Nicola was already home that afternoon when I got back from Moonee Ponds with a carload of food. Her sopping Chinese slippers were propped over the laundry trough, and the runners she had bought at Target were on her feet. She displayed them with ostentatious disapproval. I laughed.

'Did you write your article?' she asked.

'Nope. Didn't write a word.'

'What? That's really bad,' she said roguishly. 'That's naughty. You'll be telling people it's naughty Nicola's fault that you're not doing any work.'

The air in the room thickened. Keeping my eyes down, I lugged the baskets of food into the kitchen and dumped them on the floor.

'I didn't waste the day.' I heard in my voice the pathetic attempt to dodge her accusation. 'I answered some letters and made some phone calls. I just didn't write the story. I'll do it on Thursday.'

But she had already lost interest.

'Anyway my news,' she said, 'is that they've persuaded me to have the vitamin C again tomorrow after all.'

I straightened up and looked at her in silence.

'A very low dose,' she added, watching me.

'Whose idea?'

'Another doctor who came in today. He said he'd never, ever seen anyone react to the vitamin C the way I do.'

'Really. Have other people had negative reactions?'

'No—no one's had the reaction I have.'

'Yes, I understand that, but has anyone ever reported any other sort of bad reaction to it?'

'No. Nobody's ever even heard of anyone reacting the way I do.'

Take a breath. Let it pass.

'Hang on, though—isn't tomorrow your appointment with the oncologist?'

Her brow crinkled. 'Yes, but that's at half past eleven. He'll probably just run his eye over me. I'll go straight back to the clinic afterwards. If you can drive me.'

'OK. So you think you'll be right to fly home on Saturday?'

'Sure to,' she said. 'Three more days of the treatments and I'll be as fit as a Mallee bull.'

She smiled, and her eyes glazed over. I had to turn away.

~

I didn't want to go in with her, but she made me.

The oncologist Dr Maloney was a neat, slight,

friendly man in his fifties, with the springy body language one sees in modern medicos whose wives make them jog, swim, and eat low-fat cereals. He faced us pleasantly across his desk. Behind him a window gave on to a cold grey courtyard fringed by a low hedge of box. He kept his gaze strictly on Nicola's face while she spoke at length about her illness and its treatments: not once did he betray her by glancing at me. I sat beside her, exasperated, fascinated, watching the river of her trust re-direct itself and flood towards him. Did he feel it coming? Was he used to this?

'The shuddering fits,' he remarked at last, in a dreamy tone, 'sound to me like what…we…call… rigors.'

We looked at him in silence. He snapped into focus and started to scribble on a pad.

'I need an MRI and a bone scan. Go straight over to the Mercy Private. I can get you in there right away. Call me the minute you get the results.'

In the car Nicola too was dreamy.

'I like him,' she said. Her face had softened and lost definition. 'He cares about me. He's clever. Can you call Colette and tell her I won't be coming in today? Do you like him, Helen? What do you think of him?'

'Yes, I like him.' Was this all she was hungry for? A stream of sympathetic attention from a man?

~

That afternoon at the Mercy, while technicians with distracted faces took charge of Nicola, I sat on a plastic chair in the hall outside the private suites and refreshed my expertise in the scandalous lives of celebrities. Time passed without meaning. I went hunting for food and drink. I tried to be discreet in my curiosity about the patients who limped and staggered by, or were wheeled past in chairs or on gurneys. One woman, middle-aged, slim, pretty and frantic, kept pacing up and down the hall near where I sat. She collapsed on the chair next to mine, sprang up, sat down, leafed through a magazine, threw it aside and took off again along the long carpeted passageway.

Towards five, just before they called Nicola in for a bone scan, she rang Dr Maloney on her mobile to arrange to bring the test results to his rooms. She turned to me with a thrilled smile.

'He says he'll come to us. He's coming here to see me!'

Her scan was still in progress when Maloney in his good suit came bounding along the hall. I waved and jerked my thumb at the suite door. He grinned at me, and was about to take the chair next to mine when the anxious woman appeared round the corner and made a beeline for him. He got up at once and went to her side. He took her arm and made her sit down. He leaned right in towards her, almost touching her forehead with his. He pointed to her upper chest, and said in a clear, audible voice, 'Yes, Debbie—there is something there.'

Her face went blank. Then she burst out sobbing, and covered her eyes with one hand. 'Oh no. I can't do it again. I just can't.'

Very sweetly he took her other hand, still looking her right in the face, and said in a voice of passionate gentleness, 'I know. I know.'

She sprang to her feet and rushed away. He turned to me with a helpless shrug.

'Brutal, isn't it. And I have to tell her here.'

He sat down beside me and took a pad and

pencil out of his pocket.

'You need to know this. Look.' He sketched part of a spine in deft lines and curves. 'This is Nicola's vertebra C7. Know where that is?"

'Neck?'

He nodded. 'C7's been almost totally devoured and replaced by tumour. Which is now bulging out towards the spinal cord.' He cross-hatched vigorously: a crude lump almost touching a long canal of darkness. 'If something can't shrink the tumour, or if the remains of the vertebra aren't cut out and replaced with metal, she'll end up quadriplegic.'

I gaped at him.

'I won't tell her the quadriplegia part now,' he said. 'But she is not to do yoga, right? She's not to lift heavy or awkward things, or carry them. Understand?'

He shoved the pad into his jacket pocket, and looked at me with a twisted little smile.

'What about the Theodore?' I said. 'What if she wants to go back there?'

He puffed out air through his lips like a Frenchman. 'I've never met this Theodore guy, but he's given me a lotta grief. They send people on to me. The treatments in there are bullshit.'

At that moment the suite door opened and Nicola stepped out. Like a suitor, Maloney leapt to his feet. Her dazed smile of greeting faded. He put out his hand to her, and led her to a chair.

~

We drove home, stunned and silent, through peak hour traffic. As we swung on to Flemington Road she said in a low voice, 'I don't think I'll go back to the Theodore any more.'

'Good,' I burst out, jerking the wheel. 'They've brutally wasted your energy. And your money. You should demand a refund.'

She turned away. There was no point in apologising. We were both stricken, in shock. At home I scraped together a meal, and we picked at it with faces down-turned. She retired to her room with the cortisone and Panadol she had been prescribed by Maloney, and shut the door. Before long I heard her snoring: it sounded like someone choking.

I called Leo.

'C7?' He breathed in sharply.

'She's seeing a surgeon on Friday, for an opinion.'

'Who's the surgeon?'

'His name's Hathaway.'

'Hathaway! I knew him at high school. Oh, he's very good. The best.'

'Maloney says he's technically brilliant. But apparently he tends to be a bit...abrasive.'

'You'll like him, Helen. He's the Charlton Heston of neurosurgery.' He laughed. 'Those guys have to be very brave. It's a bit much to expect charm as well.'

In the night she needed me. She was sweating hugely from her head and neck. Her pillow was a puddle. I changed the bedding again and again. It was labour. It was *Let me turn the mattress*. It was *Here, drink this*, and *No, you must drink*, and *What else can I bring you?* And *Lie down now*, and *Go back to sleep*. It was hard and I was tired, but rarely had I felt so useful. I knew I only had to haul myself to the end of the week: Maloney had told us that once the cortisone kicked in for the pain she would be fit to fly home.

I would go in to the Theodore Institute and say her farewells. I would be carrying a bag full of hand grenades.

When I looked in at dawn she had run out of dry clothes and was asleep in her damp bed wearing nothing but a holey old rose pink cashmere jumper.

After breakfast I hauled her mattress into the sun, and ran load after load of sheets through the machine. She came out into the yard as I was hanging them on the line. I put down the pegs and turned to her. I was not tall enough to contain her as a mother or a husband would, but I held out my arms. She stepped into them and stooped to rest her head on my shoulder: oh, her terrible thinness. We both cried. Her hot tears ran under my collar.

'I thought I was on the mountain top,' she said in a voice that splintered. 'But I'm only in the foothills.'

All day she kept dissolving into quiet weeping. Sometimes I would put my arms around her; sometimes we would just go on with what we were doing. The hard, impervious brightness was gone. Everything was fluid and melting. There was no need for me to speak. She looked up at me and said it herself, as I put a cup into her hand.

'Death's at the end of this, isn't it.'

12

MR HATHAWAY the neurosurgeon had rooms in an old red brick house behind the Epworth Hospital. He was a large, powerful-shouldered fellow with thick hair and delicate hands that toyed, on his timber desk, with the fattest, blackest, shiniest Mont Blanc pen I had ever laid eyes on, twice the normal length and thickness of barrel, and sporting a colossal golden nib.

He did not spare Nicola.

'I've had a good look at your scans,' he said. 'If you should fall or stumble, if you jerked or jolted or twisted your neck, the lump of tumour that's replaced your C7 vertebra might collapse. And if it does, it'll squirt tumour and scraps of destroyed vertebra all over the place, in there.'

From my seat near the door, scribbling madly in my notebook with a shaking pencil, I saw her gulp and swallow. She made no other response, but sat as upright as she could, looking him straight in the eye.

'If that happened,' he went on, 'you'd immediately become quadriplegic. And that'd be the end of you.'

He told her that he was the only neurosurgeon in Australia who could put in a titanium post, as distinct from plastic or a bone graft, to replace the cancer-devoured C7. He listed for her, and I noted, the days of the week on which he operated. He told her she would have to wear a neck brace for three months after the operation. Then he shoved back his chair, and sat regarding her from under his brow, dexterously rolling the mighty fountain pen between his finger and thumb.

He lacked Maloney's sweet, almost tender style; but I could not help liking him, and I admired his merciless candour. Surely it couldn't be true though, I thought, putting away my notebook, that he was the only one who could do this procedure. It was out of the question that he should be the only one. No—Maloney would find his counterpart in Sydney and she would fly home tomorrow morning, as she had originally planned.

Nicola stood up carefully, with a small sigh. She gave him her hand, and said, 'We're going back to see Dr Maloney. We'll make a plan with him. I'll call you this afternoon.'

He got to his feet. 'I would most seriously advise you,' he said, 'not to delay.' Picking up her old-fashioned manners, he almost bowed us out.

~

Nicola climbed out of the car in front of Maloney's building and I drove on, looking for a park. I found a spot at once, but I sat in the car for ten minutes, filing my nails, full of dread. I called on the mobile a respected health journalist I knew in Sydney.

'Of course she can have the surgery up here,' she said, astonished. 'Only yesterday at St Vincent's a friend of mine had cancerous vertebrae replaced—a bit lower down the spine—three of them. Her husband told me they were very impressed with the result. You can't be expected to deal with this on your own. Where's her family?'

Her impatient toughness should have strengthened me, but in fact it gave me an urge to defend Nicola, to find excuses for her. How would anyone dare not to be impressed? Anything else would be too terrifying.

When I got to Maloney's waiting room, I found Nicola settled on a chair beside a middle-aged woman who was draped in fanciful, brightly coloured clothes. They looked conspiratorial, murmuring urgently to each other, their bowed heads bobbing and bumping. As I approached, the other woman was called in. I took her empty seat. Nicola greeted me with a hectic smile.

'That was Melanie,' she said. 'She's from the Theodore too.' She lowered her voice to a hiss. 'She was telling me about a sort of alcohol treatment that can be injected straight into the tumour. She said doctors are allowed to do it in Africa, but not here. And she said she's read on the internet about a special camera. In Russia! That might be available here, soon.'

'A camera.'

'Yeah—she says it picks up cells that are irradiated by spirulina. The only trouble is, it can't tell you whether the cells that glow are cancerous or pre-cancerous.'

I stood my bag on the carpet.

'I should go back to the Theodore, anyway,' she rattled on, shifting awkwardly on the hard chair. 'I haven't paid them for the third week yet.'

I folded my arms and closed my eyes. Let me pass out now. I want to lose consciousness. Please, Dr Maloney, take me to a hospital. Put me in a bed and spread a cotton blanket over me. Let me lie there alone in silence till this is over.

~

'Actually,' said Maloney from behind a desk that was half the size of Hathaway's, 'it is true. He practically invented this particular titanium post. If that's what you want, Nicola, he's your man.'

'Yes, Doctor John,' she said fervently. 'That's what I want. It really is what I want.'

'In that case,' said the doctor, 'you'll be having the surgery in Melbourne, at the Epworth. Probably early the week after next.'

Maloney must have seen my face drop. For a

couple of beats he sat motionless. Then he said, 'Now you two had better go home and have a brutally frank talk with each other.'

~

I hardly trusted myself to get behind the wheel. I drove in a dumb panic, stupefied; I kept grinding the gears, and could not picture the route home. We went droning north along Nicholson Street. I could feel her looking at the side of my face.

'Nicola,' I said. 'You can't have the operation in Melbourne. You've got to go home to Sydney and have it there.'

'No no no no darling,' she said, 'I want to have it here. Hathaway's the best in the country. Dr John said so.'

I raised my voice. 'Nicola. This is crazy.'

'I trust Dr John,' she said. 'If I have it here, Dr John will come to me.'

'But we don't have the back-up. There's no one here to help me.'

I glanced at her as we bounced over the railway line. She was staring straight ahead, grinning like a lunatic.

'Dr John's not like the other doctors,' she crooned. 'He really likes me—I can tell. He cares about me. I need him to look after me.'

She refused to hear me. I would have to sink the knife.

'Will you fucking listen to me?' I said shrilly. 'I. Can't. Do it.'

She sat very still.

'I paced myself for three weeks,' I said. 'I thought I could just about make it through to tomorrow. But now you're assuming I'll run the next lap as well, and the one after that. I'm trying to tell you: I'm worn out. I can't go on.'

She stared through the windscreen. I thought I might have to stop the car and throw up in the gutter.

Then she took a quivering breath, and in her noblest tones began to praise me. 'And what a splendid relay runner you've been! What a fabulous race you've run, darling. Of course you can hand the baton over. I know what I'll do! I'll rent a serviced apartment. Or I'll move into a motel.'

My palms on the steering wheel began to sweat. 'You will not, you cannot,' I said, 'move into a serviced apartment or a motel.'

'Of course I can. There must be charming places over there near the hospital. I can look after myself. All I have to do is wear a neck brace.'

'Listen to me, Nicola. This is not about a neck brace. You'll need a team of people to care for you every day, and through the night—to change your sheets and wash them, and buy food and cook it. Your family and friends will not let you move into a motel. It's not going to happen. You must go home to Sydney.'

'I'll fly home in the morning. You'll come with me, won't you. I can't fly alone. I'll organise things with Iris, and pick up a few things I'll need. Then I'll be back here next week. I have dozens of darling old school friends who live in Melbourne. They'll take me into their homes with all their hearts!'

A wave of sickening rage swept through me. I wanted to smash the car into a post, but for only her to die—I would leave the keys in the ignition, grab my backpack, and run for my life.

~

The house, from the moment we pushed open the front door, began to hum with ugly feelings. Anger and fear, rigidly suppressed, sang in the air. The fridge was empty. I rode to the shop and bought food for our lunch. As I chopped and toasted, I made an awkward twisting movement and pulled a muscle in my lower back. Even as the grunt of pain crossed my lips I flushed with shame. What pathetic rivalry, a tweaked back muscle versus a tumour that threatened to collapse and fill Nicola's body with debris and poison. But she didn't hear me. She was lying on the couch, raving in a febrile excitement.

'There's Verity,' she cried. 'And Tory and Flick, but she might have moved to Paris. Verity married that barrister who was so successful, I forget his name. They used to own a divine little cottage across the road from their house. And the au pair lived in it. I could move in there!'

'How long is it since you were last in touch with them?'

'Oh, only a few years.'

'Nicola,' I said, 'shouldn't you maybe check with Verity? To see if this is real?'

She beamed right into my face, with glazed eyes.

'Oh no, darling. I know she'd have me at the drop of a hat. She adores me.'

'But it's a twenty-four-hour commitment. Maybe she's got, you know, family responsibilities, or a job?'

She froze for a second, then clicked her tongue and made a brushing motion with one hand. She seized a pencil. 'Well, if that doesn't suit, I'll—I'll book everyone into a hotel. The Windsor. I'll take a suite at the Windsor.'

'Everyone? Who's everyone?'

She began to scribble down the names of the Sydney friends and country relatives who she *knew* would rush down to Melbourne, in shifts, to care for her. Her sister Pip would be there in a flash. Iris would drop everything and come. Clare would leave her kids in Byron and jump on the next plane south. Harriet would hoon in from Yass. Everyone would be on deck! Nicola would fly them to Melbourne, Nicola would book the tickets, Nicola would pay!

I stood at the griller, giddy with panic. 'But that'll cost—'

'Anyone who puts themselves out to look after me,' she declared with a regal gesture of her pen hand, 'deserves the best that money can buy. Now. I'll be in hospital for three days, so that means—'

'Three days? Didn't Maloney say seven to ten?'

'Nonsense, Hel. I'll be out of there so fast. OK, which were the days Hathaway operates? Tuesday and Friday?'

For this at least I had evidence. I pulled the notebook from my bag and read out in an authoritative tone what I'd written in his rooms: 'He operates on Mondays and Fridays.'

Her brow came down. She shook her head. 'No. It wasn't Monday. It was Tuesday.'

She picked up the cordless and called his receptionist. As she listened, her cheek-bones went pink. Power surged through her. She tossed the handset on to the carpet. 'I knew I was right. It's *Tuesday*.' She hauled herself upright against the cushions and hit me with a bright stare of triumph. 'By the way—while you were at the shop Bessie knocked at the door. I pretended there was nobody home.'

I put the rubber band round the notebook, limped off into my room, and lay on the bed. From there I could hear her on the phone, jabbering, bursting into fountains of laughter, organising the troops, lining up reinforcements. In a while she called to me from the hallway: she was going to take the train downtown to settle her account at the Theodore Institute. The slammed door shook the house to its foundations.

Somehow I dozed off. Soon after four o'clock there was a light tap at my window: Bessie's eyes gleamed between the blind slats. I got up and opened the front door. She stood on the mat staring up at me, the dark brim of her sun-hat pressed back off her brow like a cavalier's. She bounced straight on to my bed and we lay down. She had been thinking; she wanted me to hear the fruits of it.

'When a person dies,' she said, 'a little bit of them flies away from their body.'

'Yes,' I said. 'I've heard people say that. What a beautiful idea.'

'It's called a soul.'

She took hold of my wrist and gently moved the skin up and down over it. I felt the crepy looseness of what covered me, the fragility of the joint.

'Everyone has to die,' she said. 'Even me. Even Hughie. And Nanna, if we died, you'd die too. Because you'd be so sad.'

13

I DIDN'T know then, as Bessie and I lay on my bed and reasoned about fate and the universe, that Nicola's mad dream of flying her carers down to Melbourne and putting them up at the Windsor Hotel would come true, and that in ten days she would return to Sydney for good with Mr Hathaway's titanium post flawlessly implanted in her spine.

I didn't know yet how many times I would fly to Sydney to play my small part in the remains of her care, or how often, when I buzzed at Iris's apartment, the door would be opened by Harriet from Yass, her round, weather-beaten face sweating and wild with fatigue, or by Marion the Buddhist, white, composed and stoic after a five-day stint without relief. I had not prepared myself to sleep on the floor beside Clare from Byron, when Iris, half out of her mind, pulled on a backpack and fled north, on foot, along the coast of New South Wales.

I could not imagine the urge to start drinking that would seize me every time I entered the high, airy rooms of the apartment and found Nicola enthroned on the sofa where, propped against its hard padded arm, she woke and slept and laughed and coughed, commanding the stewing of Chinese herbs, planning brown rice fasts and drastic alkaline diets, turning her face up each morning to the sun that streamed in through the uncovered windows. Nor could I foresee that one day, with her swollen legs propped on a stack of cushions, she would announce brightly, 'I've suddenly realised why I feel so terrible—I must be anaemic.' Or how dull my life at home would seem between my visits to Sydney, how I would write to her on a postcard: 'I miss you. I'm bored. I'd rather be scrubbing shit off Iris's bathroom tiles.' For this too would be required of me: like her other carers, whom I came to love in the intimacy of our labour, I would have to help carry her to the lavatory, where I learned to wash her arse as gently as I had washed my sister's and my mother's, and as some day someone will have to wash mine.

I might have guessed that she would resist the hospice until the contents of her lungs began to bubble up into her nose and throat, until everyone around her was deranged with exhaustion, fury and despair. She relented only when Marion said to her, 'Don't regret the things you haven't done. That's the past. Let it go. Rejoice: you're our teacher now.'

But for all my anxious readiness I was still shocked by the summons. It reached me at Writers' Week in Adelaide. On the plane to Sydney everything I looked at—strangers' hair, the weave of their garments—glowed with a forceful value. When I tiptoed into her hospice room, preparing to be solemn, she took my hand with her slow, puffy one and croaked, under the oxygen cannula, 'Did you nick off from the festival? Any gossip?' I told her how the big names had scrambled to see the Nobel Laureate get his Australian citizenship in a tent, and gleeful laughter rose off her in a shimmer. Feebly she squeezed my fingers and murmured the last thing she said to me: 'Don't go, will you.'

I did not foresee that two Buddhists would chant

her out of there: that with Clare and Iris I would crouch shuddering in a corner of the dim hospice room, and listen to the thrilling alto drone of the women's voices, calling on all compassionate beings to come to that place, to come to Nicola, who like each of us in this life had been sunk deep in the mud of unbearable suffering; for whom the light of this life had set, who was entering a place of darkness, a trackless forest; who had no friends, who had no refuge, who was poised on the lip of a precipice, a frightful chasm into whose echoing spaces she would plunge and be swept away by the mighty wind of karma, the hurricane of karma. I glanced up from this scalding vigil and saw her sister's face in profile against a black curtain, patient and stark, as grand in the remnants of its beauty as was the face that lay gasping on the pillow.

Nor could I foresee that at her memorial celebration, days after her ashes had been scattered in the presence of those who had been closer to her than I, a beautifully clad woman with the order of service in her hand would address me thus, in a voice with a nasal, frosty edge: 'I'm Verity. I was at school with Nicola. I see you're to speak, and I was curious to know—what exactly was your connection to her?'

I had no idea that, before she left my house, Nicola would write me a valedictory letter of such self-reproach, such tenderness and quiet gratitude, that when I came across it, months later, in its clever hiding-place, I was racked with weeping, with harsh sobs that tore their way out of my body, as she had fancied her toxins would rush from hers. I did not know that the investigator would come to my house, that I would pour my story of the Theodore Institute into his tape recorder and never hear from him again. Nor did I guess that one evening at the end of the following summer I would pass Dr Tuckey trundling a small suitcase along Flinders Lane in the perfumed dusk; that when I saw him pause with an ungainly movement to hitch up his hopeless trousers I would pity him for the fact that all his patients must die.

The one thing I was sure of, as I lay pole-axed on my bed that afternoon beside the child with her loosening nit-plaits and her new philosophy, was that if I did not get Nicola out of my house tomorrow I would slide into a lime-pit of rage that would scorch the flesh off me, leaving nothing but a strew of pale bones on a landscape of sand.

~

That night, her last one in my house, I couldn't sleep for the tremendous snoring that sawed through the closed doors of her room and mine. I lay under the quilt with my fists clenched in an ecstasy of despair. Was it the Valium Maloney had given her? The steroids? Was it death itself playing with her, making free with her poor tired passageways and membranes? I was sick with shame, raging at myself for raging, raging at death for existing, for being so slow with her and so cruel.

But in the morning we rose in an exhausted peace. She said she was not in pain. We packed her few things in the cloth bag. I shouldered it, and picked up my own. We took a taxi to the airport, checked in, and drank a coffee there, beside a wall of glass. Across the sky a breeze combed the high, streaky clouds of spring.

The flight was short. We sat barely speaking, watching the light tremble and flutter across the silver wing. Sometimes she turned to me and smiled. Iris was waiting at the other end. When I spotted her wild hair and witty face floating in the crowd I could have gone down on my knees to her. She greeted us. I handed her Nicola's bag, and stepped back; for though our farewells when I left Iris's apartment next day were loving, though Nicola held both my hands and kissed my cheeks and looked me in the eyes, and though now the three of us walked shoulder to shoulder like sisters across the terminal to the car, I had already left my place at Nicola's side.

It was the end of my watch, and I handed her over.

PHOTO © NICHOLAS PURCELL

About the Author

HELEN GARNER was born in Geelong, Australia, in 1942. She has been publishing novels, stories, nonfiction, and journalism since 1977, when her first novel, *Monkey Grip*, appeared. She was awarded Australia's richest literary prize, the Melbourne Prize for Literature, in 2006. She lives in Melbourne.